SAVED BY THE BELL

JOSIE CAPORETTO

Dedicated to my hometown of Messignadi.
Thank you for my amazing childhood.
A special thank you to my writing friends for guiding me thought this journey, Andra Ashe & Elvina Payet.

eroporto dello Stretto. This was what Azzurra Beamondo could see from her plane window through the forehead smudge she left after the long flight. She tapped her acrylic fingernails on the armrest impatiently.

"Wonderful, I can understand the first word."

She looked around. *Why is everyone in a hurry to get up?* Azzurra didn't move, hoping she'd made the right decision. Italy was so far away from home. The excitement of her very first white Christmas and spending it in a country so rich with history helped her keep the homesickness at bay. She always felt she was born in the wrong century.

Reluctantly, she grabbed her handbag, her overnight backpack from the overhead rack, and made her way outside the plane.

Cold, icy wind blew on her face. Slowly, she went down the steel airplane front stairs. She looked for the entrance door. It wasn't the huge and elegant airport of Melbourne after all, but the provincial airport of Reggio Calabria in southern Italy.

The light cardigan she wore wasn't going to help her. She never expected the weather to already be so cold in November.

Now wasn't the time worry about this small detail. Her concentration centered on following the moving crowd to the luggage pick up.

She entered the warm room. A group of people waited on one side, greeting their arrivals. The tiniest luggage carousel she'd ever seen sat on the other side of the room. The air of Christmas was evident. Lights and adorned trees decorated everywhere the eye could see. The only thing missing was the Christmas carols.

The thought of experiencing a white Christmas excited her, but she would miss not spending that special holiday with the ones she loved.

"Signorina Beamondo?" a tall, dark, and handsome man asked.

"Yes, it's me." She paused a moment. "Please tell me you speak English." This remained one of her fears in coming to the old country not being able to communicate.

"I do. I am Santo De Angelis."

She noticed a touch of an English accent, but not a native.

"I carry this for you. Which one is your luggage?" He took her overnight backpack from her hand. "Let me guess, the pink one?"

"It's fine, I can get my own suitcase." Before she could finish her sentence, he had it already in his hand. Round muscles bulged on his upper arm with no strain at all.

She smiled. "This could be interesting," she mumbled under her breath.

"Signorina, if you please, follow me to your uncle's car. We can make our way to Messignadi and your villa."

She wasn't used to all these formalities. They made her very uncomfortable. "Please call me Azzurra."

He smiled, flashing perfect white teeth. Come here and I'll bite you softly kind of teeth, accompanied by the most gorgeous full lower lip.

2

"Are you my uncle's driver?"

"I am yours for today."

Oh yes, baby. It's been a long time. Take your mind out of the gutter.

"*Prego Signorina Azzurra.*" He opened the back door for her to sit.

"Can you please call me by my first name? I am not very formal." As she said that, she turned around. Her face almost slammed into his chest. Taking a step back, she looked at his big brown eyes. Warm and sexy.

"My name is Azzurra, please don't call me *signorina*. I'm no one special." She reached for his hand where it rested on the door handle of the car. The cold of his skin felt quite lovely under her fingertips, and she paused a moment. Gathering herself, she gently pulled him away from the door and slammed it closed. "I'm going to sit next to you, I won't be treated like royalty, because I am not."

"As you wish. As Don Vincenzo's heir, you will be treated as such by the people of Messignadi."

"Then we need to educate them, don't we?"

She watched him laugh. Everything about him oozed sexuality. He made even laughing feel incredibly hot.

"Please sit in the car before you get sick. I will have my mother to answer to." He took his coat off and gave it to her.

"I can't take your coat." she said.

"But you will."

She waited for him to sit behind the wheel. He turned on the heating and lowered the music on the radio.

"Classical," she stated.

"Vivaldi."

"The Four Seasons."

"Impressive," he said as he started to drive. "I didn't know you were a musician."

"I am not. I am a poor librarian who buried herself in books and old music."

3

"We both know you are a lot more than that."

"How long have you known my uncle?"

"All my life," he answered casually. "My mother Nunzia and her sister Cata were Don Giuseppe's helpers. Now they will be yours, of course."

She swallowed at the description *helpers*. The only helpers she was familiar with was the buffet at her favorite restaurant back home. "How long have you been his driver?"

"The driver is old Nando, but I thought one hour driving in this traffic too much for him."

"Oh my God, you know what they say about assumption. I just assumed."

"I am unaware of your knowledge of Messignadi."

"Santo, you should say it's zero." She should had done more research before leaving. "I only know a few things Old Frank translated from the letters the lawyer and the mayor sent me."

Making the trip wasn't an easy decision for her, but she needed to fix whatever they required from her and then go back home.

"That's why I am here. In time you will learn everything you need to know so you can carry on with your uncle's estates."

"All this isn't sitting right with me." A long pause of silence followed that. She hadn't felt right since she received the letter asking her to go to Italy. She didn't belong here.

"What is it that is not to your liking, Azzurra?" His tone sounded serious now.

"I never met this great uncle. I'm not sure what the history is between him and my grandfather as both my grandparents never spoke about Messignadi or anyone from their family. I only know that I don't deserve any of this." Her confession hung in the air between them, and she felt better for having said it. She watched him drive. He appeared calm, cool, and collected, and not to mention sexy as hell.

"What do you know about Italian families?"

"Not much. I had no contact with Italians until I moved in the city, and Frank and Caterina became my neighbors."

"Remember something; family is everything. Italians might hold a grudges for eternity, but when it comes to the future of their own they still look after their children."

"I wouldn't know. I lost my grandparents when I was very young. And my dad married an Irish girl. I can only compare an Australian Irish family, and from what I hear, they're nothing like Italians."

They both kept quiet for a while. Azzurra took her small camera from her handbag and started taking photos of what she could see. Mostly the sea. Shepherds with their sheep or goats. It really was a different world.

"What does your name mean?" she asked out of the blue.

"Santo means *saint* and De Angelis is *of angels*."

"So your name is Saint of Angels? I thought I had the weirdest name on earth," she said, laughing.

"Not anymore. You are in good company." He resumed driving. "In school, my friends used to tease me about my name. Your uncle once said to me, it's not the name that makes the person, but the person who makes the name."

"He sounds like he was a wise man."

"He was. And he was much respected in the village."

"Did you work for him?"

"No, I did not. I grow up in his villa. He sent me to school and treated me like his own son."

"Impressive. I didn't even know he existed until I got the letter about the inheritance. Why not leave you everything? Obviously you deserve it more than me."

She watched him smile. He seemed a man happy with his life.

"My father died when I was two years old. Your uncle gave my mother and her sister a job for life. He sent me to the best schools. Gave me so many opportunities and to travel the world." He stopped for a moment. "He left me the best gift ever. A bright future and the love like a father."

Azzurra reached for him and touched his hand. He didn't move away. He turned his hand upward and held hers.

"Brace yourself, we are about to enter Messignadi, the place your grandparents were born."

Azzurra watched from her window in fascination. Snow covered all the roofs. Even the trees were adorned. Christmas lights strung from house to house.

"I never saw so much snow in my life." She waited to see if she could get the feeling that Frank talked about feelings of belonging but so far it seemed more like watching a film, with the only difference being the protagonist was herself.

The main road narrowed until she almost feared the car wouldn't fit. She hoped they wouldn't end up like one of those memes online where the cars got stuck between two walls. But he sped away.

To her, the setting seemed like a ghost town. "Not many people around."

"It's lunch time and the village people won't miss lunch for anything." He paused. "Then they will have their siesta, and after that everyone will be on the streets socializing."

As he drove she noticed that the houses looked all old and small. Most of them had one or two concrete steps. "The houses are pretty old."

"This is the old part of the village. You will see the other side with all the new houses too."

The village church appeared on the right. As the car drove, she couldn't see all the details, but definitely she couldn't miss the bright yellow walls. So different from all the cement gray of the rest of the houses.

He kept on driving. They reached what looked like a villa. The automatic gate opened, and as they were approaching the villa, she noticed on one side far away a half-destroyed church.

"Is it there where the bell is buried?"

"Yes. What do you know about it?"

"I read that it was buried many centuries ago with the earthquake."

"That's correct."

"I think it's so exciting that they want to excavate the bell."

"I should inform you that your uncle stood against the excavation of the old bell." Santo's tone took on a serious note.

She was aware that many people were afraid of change, but why hold back on doing something like that? "Wouldn't the villagers like to see a piece of their own history?"

"By tomorrow, if the snow has melted, I will take you all around your properties." His words ended the discussion.

That sounded so strange to her, she'd never had much of her own. She would have to think hard about this and the decisions she would have to make.

CHAPTER 2

*S*anto stopped the car at the steps of the villa. The old two story villa with dark bricks and white marble all around wasn't as grand as she expected. She wanted to feel some sort of connection, but so far all she felt was appreciation. The huge verandah with white steps looked amazing. From what she could see, the villa looked big. She only hoped she wouldn't get lost in there.

"Welcome home, Azzurra."

"It's so beautiful and grand."

"Your ancestors built the villa in the 17th century. Of course, your uncle modernized the inside with the years. It only has nine bedrooms."

"Only?"

They smiled at each other. She noticed two women in their fifties approaching the car.

"Don't be taken aback. The one in gray is my mother, Nunzia, the other is her sister, Cata."

"They look friendly." She laughed.

"They don't bite. But they will feed you to death."

"Oh, I have a love affair with food."

"Then you are at the right place."

"What should I call them?"

"You can call them by their first names, or call them like I do. *Mamma* and *Zia*. It's a normal thing here in the south of Italy."

"I assume they don't speak English?"

"You assume correct. Mostly they will speak dialect, at time the mother language, Italian. When they speak softly it's the beautiful Italian. When they sound like they are about to kill someone, don't worry. It's the roughness of the dialect." He squeezed her hand as he spoke. "Get ready."

As he stopped the car, Azzurra got out to find arms around her.

"*Benvenuta a casa tua.*"

She had no idea what the two women said, but she let them guide her inside the villa.

"I need to help Santo."

"No, no no."

They spoke further in Italian, and there she was lost. They took her to the lounge where the biggest fireplace she'd ever seen crackled with a hearty fire casting a glow across the room. A pine tree almost touched the high ceiling on the right side. The decorations looked antique and gorgeous. On the other side, she spied a nativity set. She went closer to touch the green carpet adorning the nativity set and realized it was actually fresh grass.

"It's our custom to decorate the nativity set with the lichens growing on top of the trunk of the trees."

"I never saw anything like it," she said.

Then one of the women came to get her and took her near the fire. They sat her comfortably, brought a shawl to cover her shoulders, and gave her a cup of chocolate. Azzurra peeked between the two women to look at Santo.

"Get used to this. They will fuss over you. At least now we can share the love."

"I didn't understand a thing, except something about Americans?"

"That would be you."

"Me? I've never have been to America."

As he kept walking away to the stairs she yelled, "Come back here, I don't understand that."

"It's how they distinguish the ones that come from an English background."

"This is going to be so hard." She placed the hot chocolate on the coffee table, then brought the shawl closer around her shoulders. "I don't understand the language, and I am not familiar with the culture."

"You will be fine. When they feed you just eat, that will keep them happy."

Holding the shawl tight around her with one hand, with the other she picked up the cup, she tried follow him, only to be stopped by *Mamma* Nunzia.

He reappeared in a flash. "If you like, I can show you around."

"I feel a bit overwhelmed. Maybe just my bedroom for now?"

"Come with me." He guided her upstairs. "All the bedrooms are up this level. No helper's quarters, even the staff's bedroom is in here."

"Glad to hear that."

They stopped at a double door. He opened half and stepped aside to let her in first.

"Here we are; the main bedroom. It's been your uncle's room for the past forty years. It is yours now."

Azzurra went in and looked around. A huge bed covered with a blue velvety blanket took pride of place in the center. Window drapes matching the bed hung majestically on one wall. A small desk and a settee rested against the opposite wall.

"This room is bigger than my own apartment back home."

"I hope you like it," he said.

"Like is not what I had in mind. This is amazing. I would get lost in here." She laughed.

"Now let's go downstairs to eat before they start yelling at me."

"Don't you think you are a bit old to be yelled at?"

"Welcome to Italy where everyone yells to clear their lungs." They both laughed.

They entered the elegant dining room. A huge table with matching chairs filled the room. A picture of what looked like royalty in the country graced the wall. In the middle of the room, a huge chandelier cascaded so low that from the door, it looked like it rested on top of the dining table.

"Why is the table set for two?" She wasn't a genius in math, but she was capable of putting two and two together.

"Don Vincenzo never ate with the help. He would only have me to keep him company."

She started collecting the knives and forks from the table.

"Help me. Where is the kitchen?"

"This way."

She followed him and put everything on the kitchen table.

"My great uncle is dead. With all respect to his position, I don't believe in that bullshit." She turned around to look at both women. Evident shock filled their faces.

"You said we are like a family right? And we damn well behave like one by having our meals together."

Zia Cata stood with her arms open in front of the table just saying, "No, no, no."

Azzurra went closer. She hugged her then placed a kiss on her cheek. "Yes, yes, yes."

Santo held the chair for her to sit.

"That fire in your veins is definitely Calabrese," he whispered in her ear.

Azzurra turned around, her lips inches away from his. "Mine is mixed with Irish, which makes it more dangerous."

"I love danger."

"*Santo, falla u mangia.*" His mom scolded him, placing a huge plate of meatballs in the middle of the table.

"Are we in trouble?" she asked, now worried and not wanting to upset *Mamma* and *Zia*.

"You are safe. She yelled, 'let her eat.'"

The women began placing a feast on the table, just like when she was very young and her nonna cooked. For a moment she went back fifteen years, when she was about eight and her nonna would cook on Sundays.

The homemade pasta, or *Maccarruni* as they called them, were the best she ever tasted. The meatballs were so soft they melted in her mouth.

"Everything was delicious. Please thank them for me."

Their smiles told her that her compliments made them happy. She only wished she could communicate with them.

"I have to go to work now," he said, sipping his coffee. 'Have your shower, rest and I will see you in a few hours."

Suddenly she felt abandoned. Just like a child on her first day of school. "You work far from here?"

"Come near the window." He waited for her to get up and follow him. "See that cottage there?" He pointed out with his index finger. "That's where I work every day."

"It's an English cottage." At that sight, she felt a bit of her Anglo-Saxon life appeared in front of her eyes.

"I will take you around later on so you can see everything."

"Including your office?"

"You bet."

"Now go and rest. Try to shake off a bit of your jet lag if you can."

She watched him go. Once the door closed, she made her way back to the window. She watched long, strong legs walking on the white snow. Her thoughts were going to the X-rated. She remembered Frank's words. *Don't go too strong on those Messignadesi boys. They are more conservative than city guys.*

"Oh shit. I forgot to call home." She grabbed her phone from her bag. The battery displayed twenty percent. "It's enough to ring quickly."

❀

*W*arm, dark abyss, dreams, knocks... She woke up quickly sitting up in bed, for a moment disorientated as to where she was. Of course, she was in her great uncle's villa.

She could hear the two women talking to each other, but no idea why they were yelling. She got up and opened the door.

"*Devi mangiare!*" said *Mamma* Nunzia.

For the life of her, she didn't know what the women said, but it must had been very important for them to wake her up.

She looked at the smiling older woman, and smiled back.

It was like a contest about who could have the brightest smile.

She felt a fuzzy happy feeling inside, but still didn't understand what was going on.

While both were just standing and smiling, she watched *Zia* Cata, the younger sister, walking into her room. The woman opened the window, leaned half way out, and yelled. "Santooooooooo."

Azzurra didn't understand the rest. She sounded angry and ready to kill, but like her sister, her face appeared angelic. She came back to her, grabbed her hand, touching her jacket.

"Right, you want the jumper? You can have it."

One thing about her, she never been materialistic, and was known to give the shirt off her back.

"They worry about you. You have slept for so long and it's dinner time." He must have run like a gazelle for him to be in her room so quickly.

"How sweet of them. Please tell them to relax. I'm not hungry."

"In this village that's blasphemy." As he said that, he moved closer to his mother.

The two women continued chatting in their language. He pinched his mom's cheek, gave her a kiss on her forehead, and showed her to the door. Laughing, both women went back downstairs.

"Can I ask what happened?" she asked Santo.

"*Zia* Cata wanted you to change. She wants to wash your clothes."

"Oh she didn't want my jumper?" She giggled.

"They said you are very generous, and that I need to keep an eye on you," he said pointing a finger at her.

"Why is that?"

"Because you could lose your undies if you give everything away," he said, smiling.

"How do you know I am wearing undies?" she demanded, hand on her hip.

"Cheeky."

Did he go red? It looked like although he was trying to be adventurous, he just got embarrassed.

"Get dressed. We are going to have dinner, then we will go to church."

"Wow, that's a scary thought. I stopped going to church since my parents were killed. But hey, this could be interesting."

"It's not that bad. When in Rome, you know how it goes."

"Won't the roof fall on my head, you think?"

He started laughing, one of those laughs that began from

the belly. "Trust me. If it doesn't happen to all those who already go in to wash their sins, it definitely won't happen to you."

"How do you know that?"

"I am a very good judge of character." He went to the door, and turned around to look at her. "You have five minutes to get dressed. Probably twenty-five to have dinner, and then they will kick us from the villa and on our way to church."

"Five minutes?" she repeated. "It takes me that long to open my makeup bag."

"You are pretty naturally; you don't need makeup."

CHAPTER 3

*T*hey arrived at the church of Saint Nicola of Mira. The same church she saw from the car when she arrived in Messignadi. The façade painted yellow. A dark brown door, and a huge cross on the top of the V-shaped roof finished the look.

Who in his right mind would put that crappy color on the walls of a church? She wasn't going to voice her opinion.

She entered the aisle looking around. Suddenly, she felt a pinch of pride. "This is the church were both my grandparents used to come when they were living in Messignadi." The narrow church with benches on both sides. Row after row of uncomfortable looking wooden seats. Cupolas of different saints lined both the sides of the wall. Not that she knew who they were. She kept walking toward the altar. Behind the altar was a statue of a saint, with a long gray beard, one hand holding a book, the other a long rod. He wore a long white robe edged in red and gold. On top, a mantle in gold and red hung around his neck along with a thick gold cross. As she went closer, she read the name on the wall. *San Nicola Di Mira*. Saint Nicola, nothing like the Father Christmas that she knew.

Stop it you idiot, that's blasphemy. She hoped the roof wouldn't fall on her.

The biggest nativity scene she'd ever seen sprawled out on the left side of the altar. It looked like a huge mountain with little houses in between the trees and many figurines representing the shepherds.

"We will sit on the bench in the first row next to the organ," whispered Santo.

"Why?" Azzurra never liked the first row, not even at school.

"It's your family's seat. People will come to give you their regards. Will be easier for everyone."

She walked to where Santo instructed her, and sat followed by Santo.

"Where are *Mamma* Nunzia and *Zia* Cata?" She turned around to see both women seated a few rows behind.

With both hands, she gestured for them to come and sit with her. When they didn't move, she walked to them and took them both by their hands. They were the only family she had here, and she wasn't going to treat them like servants.

They both came and sat with her and Santo mumbled something.

He went closer to Azzurra whispering, "They worry that you are changing traditions and might look bad when people come to talk to you."

Turning towards Santo she asked, "Why would they come to talk to me?"

"You are a Beamondo."

Just like that. Because of her surname things were changing overnight.

The parish priest, Father Libero, visited first. She liked him straight away, not only because he could speak perfect English, but he had a good sense of humor.

She only wished her grandparents had been open about

their lives. She wondered why they went to so much trouble to hide their past.

The priest gave the service all in Italian. Azzurra had no problem sitting, kneeling, or standing. She knew the ritual, and she contributed in English.

"I'm impressed," teased Santo.

"Don't. I was sent to catholic schools, that's why I swear a lot." They both chuckled. She saw *Mamma* Nunzia pinching Santo's upper leg to shut him up.

"You're in trouble." She looked at him keeping his lips tight, but she could tell he only wanted to laugh.

At the end of the service Father Libero welcomed Azzurra officially to Messignadi. He encouraged everyone to stop and say hello to her. The younger generation all spoke a bit of English and that made her feel very welcome.

She noticed a gorgeous girl with long black wavy hair waiting near the organ. Azzurra had the feeling that she was waiting for everyone to finish before she would approach her. They kept on looking at each other and smiling.

"Hi. I am Isabella. It's lovely to meet you."

Azzurra smiled. Not only was she so pretty, she also spoke good English. "Isabella, it's my pleasure. Your English is perfect."

"Thank you. I have learned by listening to songs on the radio. I wish I could read and write too."

"I can teach you if you like, and maybe you could teach me Italian." The girls were deep in conversation, and though fatigue pulled at Azzurra, she didn't want to cut her short.

"We can do that, but after my wedding."

"You are getting married?" She looked so young.

"I am. In a few weeks." She paused. "I wanted to invite you to my wedding."

Azzurra looked at Santo, not sure what custom dictated here.

"Isabella, we both will be there," said Santo.

"*Grazie Dottore*. I better let you go, you need to rest. I see you at my wedding, yes?"

"Of course you will. Thank you for inviting me." She squeezed the girl's hands and gave her a kiss on her cheek.

Once they said their goodbyes to the bride to be, Azzurra looked at Santo. "Did you just invite yourself to the wedding?"

He laughed. How could anyone look so damn sexy this time of night? Should have been illegal. "The whole village is invited. Don't look shocked."

He helped her into the car, then opened the back door for his mother and aunty. Once he sat behind the wheel, he said, "We are one thousand two hundred and nineteen people in Messignadi. We all know each other. Unless there is a feud between the families, everyone is invited at weddings."

"This is so strange," she said, absorbing all the information. "You guys must have a reception big enough for the event."

"The custom is to invite mostly the men, unless they are close family."

She grabbed his arm. "What the hell?"

He laughed, and she frowned.

"Are women second class citizens here?"

"It's more economical not just traditional. Can I suggest something?"

"Of course you can, *Dottore*."

"I see you learned your first word tonight." He appeared amused and she was starting to enjoy her time with him. "Take everything you learn with positivity. You will find out that though many things might seem primitive to you, the people are good hearted, and they will do anything to help one another." He turned to gaze at her. "Of course there is always the exception to the rule like everywhere else."

*T*he villa sat in silence as everyone slept. Unfortunately for her, having slept most of the day, she remained fully awake. Turning on the side table lamp, she looked around the room. They told her this once served as her uncle's main room, and she could see it spoke of history. Everything was perfectly matched. The furniture of walnut wood would have been a few centuries old and in perfect condition. It gave her the feeling that she was back in time in another century. She got up and stood opposite the tall, slim mirror.

She smiled at her own reflection. "G'day," she said.

She didn't know anything about the family history, as her grandparents turned their back on their motherland and never spoke a word about it. Their English was so faultless that they never mixed any Italian words in their speech. All their friends came from many nationalities, but none of them were of Italian background. She wasn't sure what they ran away from, but if she could, she would get an answer before she went back home to Australia. She knew the secrets were in this village of Messignadi, and mainly in this villa that she now owned.

Once her grandparents passed away, and so did her father and mother, she tried to ask her Irish granny if she knew anything, but she had been in the dark as much as everyone else.

Once she got her job as a librarian in the city, she made friends with her neighbors an elderly Italian couple. Frank and Caterina. They expressed shock at first when they learned she had Italian background, but she knew nothing about their culture. Then they took her in like the daughter they never had. They were the ones who had pushed Azzurra to come to Messignadi and find out for herself about her heritage.

She plugged her phone into the only socket she saw near the bed, then went on social media, looking what friends were doing back home. She exchanged a few messages with her girlfriends, who told her they missed her already. Mostly they told her not to fall in love with some wog boy and stay there.

It had been such a long time since she fell in love. She had given him all of herself. A very naive country girl in a big city, afraid of the big bad wolf, and sad to find out the love of her life had been the big bad wolf. She had loved, suffered, and changed. No more naïve Azzurra. The pain had taught her survival.

Because of that horrible experience, she wouldn't give a chance to anyone else, love wasn't for her.

She had to admit the doctor in the house was pretty hot. When she told her best friend, she suggested that she should fall down the stairs to get home visits.

Her thoughts went to his gorgeous smile, the way he made her feel comfortable. His resistance to her decision to bring the old bell out ruffled her, though. It was too early to think of anything intense. She would take the time to get to know him, and then she would consider the decision.

She switched the phone off and tried to sleep. She couldn't be awake all night and be a zombie in the morning. Azzurra already knew she would have to see so many people, and start to make decisions.

Of course, sleep wouldn't come easily. Her thoughts went back home to her neighbors, the relationship they developed over the years and the trust she had in them. Then her mind went to the night they read the letters that were sent from Italy. Letters that were responsible for her being in Messignadi and this villa.

Australia six months prior

*T*he envelope looked well sealed and it was internationally registered. She could see it had come from Italy from the stamp. Feeling confused, she put a knife in and she slashed it open. The formal letter looked like a legal document. The only thing she could understand was her name.

She wasn't going to dwell on this. She stuffed it back in the envelope, and went straight to the unit next door.

"Azzurra, come in," said Caterina, her neighbor. "Dinner is about ready, you come just in time."

"Frank, look who's here for dinner."

"Azzurrina, Azzurretta we are having *pasta parmigiana* and *cotolette*," said Frank.

She knew now that the dishes were pasta with eggplant and schnitzel. Since she moved to the city, they had become her surrogate parents. While Caterina would feed her, Frank the intellectual engineer would tell her stories of his homeland.

"Frank, I just received this. It looks like two different letters, but I am not sure what they are."

Frank took the envelope, had a quick look, and brought it up to his heart. "*Fratelli d'Italia, l'Italia se desta.*"

While he sang the Italian national anthem, Caterina started yelling at him. "Frank, read the letter instead of acting like a child."

"You have no feelings, woman. This letter come from the motherland."

"Just read it," she said while stirring the pot. "Azzurra, set the table for three, darling, so we can have dinner while Frank decides to read the contents of the letters."

"Azzurra, don't listen to her. This looks like important business."

"Frank, read it," she yelled while getting the pasta out.

They watched him as his face expression changed with each

line. When he finished, he got his glass of wine, raised it, and said, "To Azzurra finally claiming what is rightfully hers."

"Which is?" she asked, now curious.

"Your grandfather had a brother in their home village. He never got married and since he died, and no any other relative is alive but you, you are the heir to all of his possessions."

"What? A pig and a goat?" Azzurra laughed.

"A little bit more than that. His villa with all the land attached. The olive farms. The old convent. The olive oil mill with all the pressed oil. The collection of cars. The shares he had invested in Italy, Switzerland, and America. And all his cash money which they don't say how much."

"Come again, Frank?" she said, shocked.

"Azzurra, you are the heiress of his patrimony, and they need you in the village."

"What village?" she asked.

"Messignadi, where your family is from."

"Why do I need to go there?"

"For a few reasons. The first so you can claim your patrimony, which is the legal document from your uncle's lawyer. The other letter comes from the mayor. He needs permission for an old bell of nearly five hundred years to be excavated from your land to be put in the village church."

"Five hundred years? Frank, that's amazing."

Frank pulled his chair out, then sat at the head of the table still holding the letter. "Can you believe this, Caterina, the money didn't interest her, but that old piece of junk does."

"Think about it. This bell is older than my own country." Azzurra's curiosity spiked.

She reached for her iPhone, and searched online for Messignadi and its bell. "Look, the bell was buried after an earthquake many centuries ago." She scrolled down the blog.

"He left his patrimony to you. You are rich. And you worry only about an old bell."

"Fuck me dead." That's all she could come up with.

CHAPTER 4

*W*aking up in a silent house became a thing of the past. The female voices could be heard from upstairs. At first, Azzurra thought they were fighting, and then suddenly she could hear laughing. She didn't bother getting dressed. She wore the woollen robe *Mamma* Nunzia gave her, and made her way downstairs following the voices.

Three ladies, probably in their early seventies, were standing chatting away. Where was the logic in that? Why not sit down to chat? The moment they saw her, they went to hug her. She wasn't sure what the hell to do as the feeling of being attacked by the huggers crossed her mind.

They spoke loud and fast, and Azzurra understood only their laughter. That was universal.

Mamma Nunzia made the presentations. For that she didn't need a translator.

"*Comare* Rosina, *Comare* Teresina, and *Comare* Fortunata."

Mamma grabbed her hand and took her to the settee. She watched as the visitors gave her a present, each wrapped in brown paper, then took a place near her.

"Thank you, *grazie*."

She kept on smiling back at them, not sure that else she was supposed to do. Between sign language and grins, she understood that they wanted her to open the presents. Confusion engulfed her. Each parcel had a packet of sugar and one of coffee.

There must have been a perfect explanation why they gave her this particular gift. She only wished she knew.

They started asking her questions. They were waiting for an answer, but she had zero idea how to continue the conversation.

She'd watched the *Godfather*. They probably wanted to know some gossip. What else would old women have in a small villages?

Sipping her coffee, eating the fresh pastry *Zia* would pass to her, she tried to understand the quick words that they were saying. At times she would look quickly outside through the window, wondering how busy Santo was in his office. She knew it wasn't protocol to just get up and leave her visitors, so she stayed there, bored out of her wits while her cheeks were sore with how much smiling she was doing.

She needed a good excuse to be able to get up and leave the scene. Bingo, the coffee cups, she would have to wash them and that alone would excuse her from the obligatory chit chat.

She walked to the sink, placed the pretty cups in, then wrinkled her nose as a strong smell permeated the air. A noise made her turn around, and she let out a scream.

"What the fuck!" A scene she'd never seen before in her life played out on the table. Two chickens, tied up together by their feet, flew about on the table. On instinct she grabbed a kitchen knife, and though scared of the chickens, she went to them. With trembling hands, she cut the cord that bound them together.

"Azzurra, *che succede?*" asked *Mamma*.

She hoped she asked if everything was okay. Everyone else stood behind *Mamma*.

"Those poor little chickens were being abused under my own roof."

Both chickens ran from the table to the floor, and everywhere in the room.

She saw the looks the women were giving her, probably thinking she was crazy.

Santo entered the kitchen, wearing his white coat and looking so damn sexy. How in the hell could anyone look so delicious this early in the morning?

"What's wrong?" he asked going to her and taking the knife from her hands.

"The chickens were taken hostage; I had to free them." She couldn't keep still. She had to see where the chickens were running off to.

"I didn't think you were a vegetarian."

"I'm not, but I've never seen chickens alive on a kitchen table fighting for survival before."

She watched two of the women getting the chickens back with the skill of a samurai, then they took them outside while laughing.

"Whose chickens were they?"

"That's your dinner," he replied as if that was the most normal answer ever.

"Excuse me, my what?" She could almost feel her eyes falling out of their sockets.

"Being a doctor in a small village doesn't mean they pay you always with money. Look in the pantry. Sometimes they give you what they can." He turned around and opened the pantry door. "Everything is fresh, as you can see. That's the payment I get from some of them."

"They pay you with eggs, vegies, and chickens?"

"Sometimes they bring a lamb too, but already cooked."

She looked at him for moment. "I never met anyone like you."

"You already noticed how much I eat?" he said jokingly.

"No, that's not what I meant. You are a good soul."

"I believe in karma. I would be in the street if it wasn't for your uncle's protection. That's why I am trying to give a little bit back."

"I feel so selfish right now." She couldn't find anything else to say beyond airing her guilt over her inheritance.

"I'm sure you have many good qualities. You have the same blood as your uncle in your veins."

She turned a bit too quick perhaps as she found herself in his arms. Her hands rested on his broad shoulders while his hands were on her hips. Through her thick clothes, she could feel the warmth of his touch. Neither spoke, they just looked at each other. She could feel his breath on her face and their lips almost touching. She closed her eyes for a moment. Azzurra waited, unsure for what, but knew she wanted to kiss him. She opened her eyes quickly when she heard him say, "I better go back to work, I will see you at lunch."

"Are you running away from me?" she asked.

"The little angel on my right shoulder is telling me to go, leave her alone."

"What about the little devil on your left shoulder?"

"Azzurra, we better not play with fire. We need to concentrate on the issue in front of us. I need to help you out, not take advantage of you."

"We won't have time to get burned. As soon the bell is out of the ruins, I will be back in Australia."

His face changed expression as he stepped back to look at her. "I would reconsider hard before you make such a decision."

"About going back home?"

He shook his head, then responded, "This is also your home, but I am talking about the bell. If you give permission to dig it out, you will be making a colossal mistake."

"I'm surprised that you don't see that as a positive step."

"This is not Australia. We do things a bit different here." He turned to go towards the door. "We will continue this later, now I have to go back to work."

She wanted to keep him there a bit longer, but knew he needed to go.

*S*he rushed to her bedroom where she dived onto her bed and grabbed her iPhone. She activated the video call and waited until it was answered.

"Azzurra, what a pleasure seeing you live."

"Hi Frank, I miss home. I miss you and Caterina." She felt like crying.

"What's wrong darling?" asked Caterina, popping her head in front of the camera.

"The doctor doesn't approve of the digging of the bell." Her voice deflated.

"Did you ask him why?" Caterina sked.

Before Azzurra could answer, Frank took primary position in front of the webcam. "Have you asked him why he has reservations?"

"It's complicated. I need to know more, but he went to work and said we'd talk later."

"Talk to him, understand why. Only then can you give him your point of view. At the end of the day it's your property and you can decide what you want to do."

"You know how much I love history, and it sounds like this could be a perfect opportunity for the village." She paused a bit then asked, "What exactly did the letter say?"

"In the property where the villa is, there is an old convent attached to it."

"It's opposite, not attached. What else?"

"It was half destroyed by the earthquake in 1783. They want

29

to dig out the huge bell. Apparently, your uncle had promised to sell the land attached to the convent. He never signed any paper. Now they can't do anything unless you sell them the property."

"Oh fuck, Frank. I don't know anything of this country, I don't speak the language and I know nothing of their culture. But one thing is sure; I will not sell anything."

"Just give it a bit of time, you will find your feet."

"I miss home. I don't want any of this. I just wanted to help the village regain their history."

"*Y*ou wanted a purpose in life didn't you?" he asked.

"Maybe I should quit while I am ahead."

"No. You have the Calabrian blood in your veins. You're not a quitter." He paused a moment. "Take your time. Research the motivation of this project and why the doctor is against it. Now give me one of those bright smiles before you go."

CHAPTER 5

*A*zzurra followed Santo into the villa's library where Don Vincenzo had many meetings through his life. A huge mahogany desk sat at the back wall. A built-in bookshelf climbed from wall to wall, full of books. She had died and gone to book heaven.

"Many are in English," she heard him say.

"I am so happy to see that he loved books as much as I do."

"Please take a seat." He waited for her to sit on the Chesterfield sofa, then sat on the single seat opposite her. "For the next few weeks we will be busy with lawyers, then the situation with the mayor."

"When I received the letter from my uncle's lawyer, I considered turning the offer down. When he read the one from the mayor about the bell, being a history buff, I had to come."

"I see," he said not giving anything else.

"Yes, the one that was buried with the earthquake a few centuries ago. He wrote that they wanted to recover the bell to put it next to the first one. Apparently, my uncle promised to sell the surrounding land."

"Son of a bitch!" Santo's face turned red with anger. "Can I please read the letter he sent to you?"

"Let me get it. I have a feeling that I wasn't told the truth about this." She got up and left the room, returning a few moments later with a folder.

"In here I have all communications from my uncle's lawyer to the mayor." She handed the folder to Santo and she sat waiting while he read.

"I am trying to find the right words here, Azzurra," he said while shuffling the papers in his hands.

"Don't sugar coat. Please tell me what's going on."

"The bell does exist. Two of them were from the chapel of the convent opposite the villa. The earthquake destroyed half of the convent and the bells got buried underground." He paused for a moment, enough to let her absorb what he was telling her.

"In 1808 the people of Messignadi excavated the first bell. The villagers call it the Younger Sister which is still in the campanile of the church. The other was never recovered. It's believed to be far down." He handed the folder back to her.

"The campanile is quite too small, another bell won't fit." said Santo.

Azzurra looked at him, then started to read between the lines. "Have I just walked in into a nightmare?" Suddenly, her gut feeling told her the mayor had a hidden agenda.

"He tried for years to buy the land from your uncle. His plan is to build a train rail to have easy access from Messignadi to any other village out there."

"I get the feeling my uncle didn't approve of any of this, and neither do you."

"This is your decision, you do what works for you."

She hadn't been a city slicker all her life. She'd grown up in a remote town and knew the consequences a decision like this could have on the people who lived there. "My question is, why send me a bogus request?"

"You don't need me to answer that, do you?

"Of course *not*! That asshole thought, what would she know and care? She will see the money and she will be history.'" She got up and started pacing the room. "You see things like this make me angry."

"You don't need to be angry. You have the power and the decision is only yours."

"I still believe the bell can be taken out by us, and the village won't lose anything, and neither do we."

"Azzurra, digging the bell is not a good idea either way. The village is fine the way it is."

"I can see that selling the land is not something that my uncle would do."

"He wouldn't dig the bell either. None of the Beamondo ever did."

"Give me one good reason and I will think about it," She said, now more than ever convinced that she wanted to dig that bell out.

"I can't give you two thousand years of history in a moment."

"I am a fast learner. Something as old as the bell, it's a piece of important history that needs to be seen.

"This is not like where you come from. Some things are better left unchanged."

"The mayor also asked to buy the land in Oppido for the council if I am not wrong."

"You are not wrong. That land would give him accessibility from Messignadi." He placed the folder on the desk. "We must go to the mayor's office. They will want to talk to you about the project. I am sure they are in a hurry to have everything settled."

"What are your thoughts on that?" she asked. Something told her to trust in him.

"I can give you my thoughts, but you need to make your own decision." He paused for a moment. "If you decide to go ahead, you can be one of the wealthiest women in Italy."

"Good thing I'm Australian. While money is a necessity, it doesn't make you happy. I have a funny feeling about this."

He placed both hands on her shoulders. "There is not right or wrong here, you need to decide what's right for you."

"Even if you don't agree with my decision?" she asked.

"Because I don't agree it doesn't mean I will bully you into changing your mind."

"Okay, let's pretend you had to be the one making this decision. What would you do?"

"Like your uncle, I would turn them down. They don't want to buy the land in here to excavate the old bell, or the land in Oppido to build more houses. They want the monopoly of the land. Destroy what's around and have freedom to import and export what the hell they like."

The passion she heard in his voice made her realize that though she wasn't aware of those reasons, she was right not to trust this process. "I didn't want to come to Messignadi. I never knew my *Zio,* I never heard of him, therefore I don't feel I deserve any of this. You, on the other hand, were the son he never had, you were there for him until his last breath. You deserve his patrimony."

"I have a degree that gives me a good income thanks to him."

"Looks like you only take chicken and eggs for payment."

They both laughed at that.

"He thought of me too in his will, as you are aware, and the rest is rightfully yours. Now I should go before they think I skipped town." He got up and went closer to her. "You better rest now."

For a moment they just stared at each other, neither speaking.

"We better keep this realistic." She had no intention of taking home a husband.

She watched him leave, and of course she ran to the window to watch him until he disappeared into the medical cottage.

❧

*A*zzurra could appreciate the fact that Santo was against the idea of selling the land, he had grown up there after all. What wasn't clear to her was why he didn't agree with digging the bell up. Boots, hat, and coat on, she made her way out. As she opened the front door, a blast of wind welcomed her. Straight in her face. It had snowed during the night. Her first instinct was to lie down on the white cold blanket and make a snow angel. She had never seen so much snow before. Now wasn't the time to discover the fun. She was on a mission.

From the kitchen window the convent didn't look that far. It wasn't close either. Following the path, she walked towards the half-ruined building. Olive trees were all around the property. She felt pride in her ancestors who had the vision.

"I wonder how I would have been as a person if I had been born in these lands." She would never have that answer. Her destiny took a different path.

Arriving at the destination, she stopped to look at the old, ancient, and enchanted convent. The walls still standing looked like solid rock, no doors of course. She walked to where she thought the bell tower used to be. Only a rock here and there indicated the previous existence of the left wall.

"So the bells must have fallen under here," she said to no one in particular.

"Almost there, a bit higher."

"Fuck me!' she screamed, whipping around so hard she almost injured her neck.

"Where in the hell did you come from?" No, she wasn't complaining about the doctor following her. No woman in her right mind would complain, but he scared her out of her wits.

"I saw you walking towards here. I tried ringing you on your cell phone and I've been calling you." He looked worried.

"The phone is on silent, and I was too engrossed with reaching the place. I didn't hear you calling."

"I would rather you ask someone to walk with you when you want to explore your properties."

"I have travelled half the world on my own to reach here." Did he intend to start treating her like a poor little female? No, she wouldn't accept that from any male. Not even the hot take-me-now doctor.

"It has been snowing all night and it's slippery. The convent is a danger zone." Santo walked to one of the rocks, gave it a light shake, and it fell down. "Unless you know where to walk or touch, it could be dangerous. I wasn't playing the macho man; you don't need me to save you."

Describing the moment as awkward was an understatement for Azzurra. "I wanted to see where the old bell is."

He took her hand. "Come with me."

She didn't let go. Hands together, fingers locked, they walked along.

"This is exactly where they excavated the bell, and it's believed the Big Sister is down there."

"So no one knows for sure?"

"The way the bells were put together, they fell one after the other." There was no other explanation.

"I suppose we'll find out once we start the work."

"Azzurra, your decision to excavate the bell won't be welcomed by the villagers. It's been down there for a long time."

She could tell he was growing angry, but tried to keep calm.

"You can't afford to have everyone turning on you. While they need you to keep their jobs, you need them to do the work." He freed his hand from hers and stood opposite her, legs apart, his arms now crossed on his chest.

"I need to know why, *Dottore*, why are they so against this?"

"The legend of the bell is sacred for the people of Messignadi."

Now it started to be a bit clearer they were attached to a legend.

"Please don't tell me, you as educated as you are you, believe in the legend?"

He shook his head. She kept on staring at him.

"You have two choices, you either believe or you ignore." He squatted near where the bell was buried, and grabbed a fistful of dirt. "Sometimes having faith in something is not the end of the world."

She walked closer to him. Chill crept into her fingertips, causing a burning sensation. She put them in her pockets, swearing never to forget her gloves again. "I wish you could see my point of view," she whispered.

"Yes, I get it. You are a visionary."

"This could be something positive. Everyone could benefit from this. Tourists could come and visit the village attraction."

"What the people of Messignadi benefit is from the bell being their sentinel."

"What do you mean?" She didn't understand why. The bell couldn't benefit anyone while underground, right?

"For many generations, some people heard the bell ring every time an accident happened." He got up, putting his hand in his jeans. "Many lives have been saved because of the bell."

"Have you ever heard her ringing?"

"I haven't, but I do believe that it happens when it's needed."

"I stopped believing in Father Christmas when I was in grade one." She wasn't going to laugh in his face, but this bullshit about the bell ringing from the ground was just a tale with no sense.

"So we shall agree to disagree?"

"It appears that way."

They both walked together, neither speaking. She made her way towards the villa while Santo walked towards his medical clinic.

CHAPTER 6

They drove to the nearby village, where the council office was. They both got out of the car.

"You are okay?" Santo asked.

She nodded.

"They all speak English. Listen to what they have to say, then make your own decision."

"How much do you trust them?" she asked.

"Not much, I am afraid. But as I said, you are intelligent enough to decide what is right or wrong for you."

For a moment their eyes locked. A feeling of fuzziness engulfed Azzurra. She knew it had nothing to do with being celibate for a very long time, but everything to do with the gorgeous man she had standing next to her.

They entered the gate, then the thick huge door. They walked through a very long hallway. Picture frames of what looked like politicians decorated the walls. The only one she recognised was the one of the Pope.

They came to a door.

"Are you ready?" he asked her.

"As ready as I ever will be."

Her mind went a hundred miles a second. How many people would be at the meeting? Then her thoughts shifted to the tall, dark, and handsome man who stood with her. She couldn't understand why he was still single, but then again people could ask her the same question. She laughed mentally. Her sense of humor was warped sometimes. He rested his hand on her shoulder and she turned around, both looking at each other. For a moment neither spoke. She wanted to scream *kiss me kiss me*, but instead her thoughts were interrupted by his velvety voice.

"Do not worry when we go in there."

She nodded at him.

"You do what's right for you. Whatever your heart tells you to do, you do."

She nodded again.

"I am here with you; don't forget it."

As if she could. She'd never been too shy to tell a man she liked him, but with Santo she couldn't do it. She wanted him to like her. She felt like a little girl with her first boy crush.

Santo knocked at the door, then they both went in.

Three men stood near the desk first, dressed impeccably in elegant suits. Their faces not very friendly. They were meeting for business, not to make friends. Santo introduced her to everyone. Mayor Masini, his lawyer Nandini, and his secretary Fonte.

Paperwork covered the desk, and she spied her surname on some of the documents. She was sure they had everything ready for her to sign.

They showed them to seats and offered coffee. Their conversation revolved around nothing. They probably thought they would make her feel at ease, but instead the whole fiasco irritated her. "Should we start? Your mother and aunty are waiting for me this afternoon to take me out visiting."

"I thought you would bring your lawyer with you," said Mayor Masini.

"Signorina Beamondo thought of listening to you before involving the legal aid," said Santo.

"There is not much to talk about it. We sent a copy of the contract to Australia, we just need a signature and it's a done deal," the mayor responded.

She wasn't going to let them play her, she wasn't stupid. "With all due respect. I need to know what is that I'm signing. I need to know why you made me come here." She paused a moment then continued, "What are your plans?"

Four men looked at her, three with murder on their mind for sure, and one with the biggest smile of approval.

"Your uncle had the same vision as us for many years," said the mayor.

"Yet he never signed and never sold his land to you. That's a bit peculiar, don't you think?" She wasn't going to hold back.

She'd heard of this mayor from the young people of Messignadi. He'd promised improvements for decades. The roads were still in bad conditions. In summer they only had water for a few hours in the afternoon. People didn't like him, and sounded like they didn't vote for him, but nonetheless he had won the elections again.

"You're from a big city. You should know that projects take time." He brought the contract to her and continued. "Sign here, *Signorina*. Your uncle had a vision and it would be a sacrilege not to do his wish."

"Mayor, you're not explaining anything to me. My uncle is gone, dead. Now all of his possessions belong to me." She grabbed the contract from his hands and shoved it back onto the desk. "You need to deal with me now. You need to explain to me what is that you want, and what your plans are, because all this chitchat is giving me a headache." She raised her hand up and looked at her nails. "To make things worse I can't even find a place to fix my nails. A woman can't deal with anything unless her manicure is immaculate." She smiled at them.

"Please, let's not waste each other's time, and let's cut to the chase."

"Very well, *Signorina*, since you are from the city you do things in a different way. Here in Calabria, women know their place."

At that Santo laughed. "We all know she's got Beamondo blood running in her veins. No Beamondo woman ever shuts up."

"Well, with all due respect, Mayor, I never married because I never wanted to be anybody's puppet. I am my own woman, and if the women of your town haven't got a voice it's not my problem. I'm an Australian and I will tell you exactly what I think." She got up, hands on her hips and continued, "Now stop wasting my time. If you want to do business with me, lay down the cards, tell me what your plans are, and if your plans meet with what I want, then we can go ahead."

She wasn't going to let them play hard ball. She already had a bad feeling about them, and not only because of what Santo and the villagers said to her, but she could smell their greed for money. No, she wasn't going to help them get richer.

"Messignadi is a proud village, but still is missing out on many things. There is no high school, no train. With your uncle's land, we can offer all those options for everyone. But most important, that bell could be the treasure of the village.

"There are lots of olive trees around, which means they all belong to me now that my uncle died."

"Yes, of course," he said.

She turned around, looking at Santo. "How many people do I have working for me?" she asked.

"Between the women who pick the olives and the man working all the land, you have about five hundred people working for you."

She looked at the mayor, and slowly she said, "Let me understand something. I have five hundred people working on

42

my lands. Once we cut the trees and we put rails in, what will happen to those people?"

The three men looked at each other. None of them spoke. Then the mayor coughed, and said, "The men will be working on the railways. They will be busy for at least a few years."

"You see, where I come from, people can get a payout, but that money doesn't last long. Once the money is finished, how are they going to put food on the table? Who's going to look after their families?" She stopped for the moment, then said, "I'm freezing my tits off here, can you turn the heater on? I don't understand why you people don't warm up the room when you're waiting for somebody to come for a meeting." She turned around, looked at Santo, hands on the hips. "Fuck me dead, do I have to tell people that it's bloody cold in here?"

She watched Santo laughing, and one of those men rushed to turn the heater on.

"Now, let's go back to this. I have no intention of signing anything. My uncle never signed because he didn't believe in this project. And neither do I."

The mayor drew closer, grabbing her upper arm. She saw Santo jumping in about to grab the mayor. With her free hand, Azzurra stopped Santo, then she loosened the mayor's fingers one by one.

"Never touch a woman unless she wants to be touched." She grabbed her bag. "The meeting is over."

"This is your doing," one of the men accused Santo.

"I can honestly tell you I am proud of her, a true Beamondo. But I can guarantee you under that beautiful hair she has a functional brain."

"I will suggest you think about this. It's a good project. Don't cut off your nose to spite your face. You can go back to Australia a very rich woman." The mayor just wouldn't give up.

Azzurra looked straight into his eyes. Slowly, she said, "Money doesn't bring happiness. I never had money and I do not care about money." She pointed towards Santo. "You see this man? He's the one who was a son to my uncle. He's the only one who was there since childhood and loved him like a father. Everything should have gone to him not me. I'm not going to sell my soul to the devil for a few dollars."

"I beg to differ, *Signorina,*" said Fonte. "We are not talking about a few dollars here, we talking about millions. You could be a filthy rich woman and have the world at your feet."

She turned around, looking at him. "I'm not a religious person. I almost never go to church, but I noticed something in church the other night. Saint Michael had something under his feet. The devil's head. I want to be like Saint Michael. I step on the devil." Her anger swelled. She'd tried to keep her cool for too long, but now she would give them a piece of her mind. "We don't have anything else to say. I won't feel good about myself if I get my people out of a job for a few pennies. But I think before I leave Messignadi, I will leave my own mark like my uncle did before me, and his father did before him, and so on. I'm an Australian. Half of my blood is Irish, but the other half is Italian. Calabrese. So let's see what I can do for my own people, because I sure as hell see you're not doing much. The kids don't even have a playground to play, and you think bringing a train will help them?"

She went closer to Santo and grabbed his hand. "Let's go, Santo, I've had enough of this bullshit."

Santo followed her. She felt her blood rushing through her arteries because of the excitement of what went on in the Mayor's office. She turned around, extending her hand to him. He grabbed it, then they walked in the cold corridor in silence. Cold wind welcomed them when they stepped outside.

"You were amazing. I came thinking I had to protect you, but I almost had to protect them from you." They both laughed.

"Do I deserve a kiss?" she asked.

He didn't answer. He brought her closer to him, holding her tight, placing his lips to hers. Slowly, he gave her the kiss she had asked for. He started nibbling at her lower lip. Once she opened them more, he found his way in with his tongue, caressing every inch of the inside of her mouth. She brought her arms around his neck and kissed him back. Matching his movements. Slowly, faster, strong and passionate.

Once the kiss broke, he opened the car door for her.

"Please sit down before I get in trouble, and we end up in prison for indecent exposure."

"For just a kiss?" she asked.

"You have no idea how close minded some people can be."

Azzurra sat and watched Santo walk in front of the car, open the door, and sit behind the wheel. He placed his strong hands on top of the wheel. He sat there for a few minutes, unmoving.

"You know that feeling when you do something that you wanted to do for a long time, but you are not sure if you did the right thing?" he asked.

"No." She paused and looked him in the eyes. "I never do anything that I don't want too. You have regrets for kissing me?"

"No, of course not. I wanted to do it from the first moment I saw you at the airport."

"Then explain what?"

"I don't want to take advantage of you. You are ten years younger and still impressionable, and I am supposed to guide you with a clear mind, not bring out my animal instincts."

"Santo, you need to know a few things about me. I am my own woman. If I didn't want your kiss, you can rest assured it wouldn't have happened." She moved a bit closer, and kissed him on his cheek.

"Now let's go home and we can talk about the rest later."

*A*zzurra called Frank giving him the news about meeting the major.

"I tell you it was like a scene from *The Godfather*, they wanted to look intimidating."

"And did they?" asked Frank.

"Hell no, they looked and acted like assholes."

"That's my girl."

"Santo and my uncle were against this project too, but today he stood back. He let me do the talking."

"He's a very intelligent man, the doctor. He wasn't going to push his view on you. I respect that."

"I don't know what the plan is next, Frank. I have to talk to him, and I want to meet the workers. I feel they should know that their job is secure."

"I think that's a very good idea. Now that your great uncle died they must be worried."

Azzurra had heard many concerns in the village, but she made sure they knew that nothing would change. Even when she would go back to Australia, their lives would be the same.

She knew that Santo was the only one who could take care of the people in Messignadi, and she could be happy knowing that a man of integrity would take care of everything.

The subject of the bell continued to loom over them, though. They both tried to stay away from that topic. A part of her felt guilty for not believing the legend.

"I better go, Frank. Give Caterina a kiss from me."

*T*he shared and acknowledged attraction between her and Santo made her happy. Yes, they had their differences about the excavation of the bell, but everything else was so organic. She would have to go home eventually, but she wasn't going to stop whatever might happen between the two of them.

She knocked at his office door very lightly.

"Come in, Azzurra, I am finishing some paperwork to send to the capital, then I'm finished for the night."

She sat on his desk, hands next to her thighs, legs dangling. "I can wait until you're done."

"Perfect, you are telling me this while you wear a short skirt, sitting next to me, and not even aware that you are tempting me."

"I am wearing my heavy stockings." She laughed.

"You are not helping me." His smile appeared warm and inviting.

She jumped off the desk. "Is there anything I can do to occupy my time?"

"You could do the filing for me."

"Deal."

"I spoke with Father Libero. Did you know in Messignadi we have one hundred and forty-five children under twelve years old?"

"I wasn't aware of the exact number," he said.

"I would like to give them all a small present for Christmas," she said.

"To all the children?"

"Yes, of course. We could have a party for them a few days before Christmas, and we could give them the present. Also, I want to assure the workers that the land won't be sold."

"We would need to think of a location," he suggested.

"All taken care of. We can use the school hall."

"What I admire about you is you're interested in learning about the culture and your interest in Messignadi," stated Santo

"I feel this experience has been a blessing in my life."

"I must admit, I had a look at your social media. It's very

clear you miss your city life. You always embark on a different adventure, and I can tell that you are like no one else I ever met. You have your quirky side, your sweet side, and I saw firsthand your *I take shit from no one* side. Your street wise intuition is amazing."

"I do miss my normal city life."

"How about I take you dancing?"

"My kind of dancing or your kind of dancing?" She let out a laugh.

"I promise tonight your kind of dance."

"Oh God, you have no idea how much I'm missing dancing."

Excitement zinged through her at the prospect of dancing with him. Azzurra would boogie her ass off all night long, and show him how much fun she could be.

※

*S*he made her way upstairs. Her plan was simple. Shower, dry her hair, make up, and then she would think what to wear. Nothing too fancy, it was a night club. She chose a pair of black pants and a silver top. Simple but stylish.

She went downstairs to give *Mamma* Nunzia and *Zia* Cata a big hug and a kiss on the cheek. And off they went.

"How far is it?" she asked.

"We are going back to Reggio Calabria, the capital city."

"You're not taking back to the airport are you?" She laughed.

"Definitely not. We are going to the *Lungo Mare*. There is a group of nightclubs we can choose from."

Excitement filled her when they arrived and she saw some of the guys from Messignadi, but of course none of the girls. This was one thing she couldn't understand. While the men could go out gallivanting, the girls would have to stay home and do some domestic thing that their mother asked them too.

"Don't look so disappointed, you will still have fun, I promise you," he said, smiling.

"Yes I know, but it would have been nice to see some of the girls from home too."

"Messignadi is still a bit traditional in that sense. Like I said before, take all the good stuff you like and don't put much emphasis on the rest."

"Yes I know."

She missed her girls. She missed being crazy with them and doing shots. But she was having an absolute blast with Santo.

"Hey, you can dance!' she said, laughing.

"You never know, I might change careers and became a professional dancer." He laughed.

The boys joined them and they all danced until her feet were sore.

The silence of the early morning hours greeted them when they reached the villa and Santo walked her to her room. She turned around and caressed his face. "Thank you, I had an amazing night."

"I had a fantastic time too."

She went closer and gave him a kiss on his lips. A very soft kiss.

He stood there and didn't kiss her back. That confused her. After the night they had, she expected a bit more.

"You didn't like it?" She took a step back and waited for him to say something.

He looked at her silently with one hand inside his jeans pocket and the other on the door frame. She waited. He smiled.

"Go to sleep, Azzurra, I am not going to kiss you at this hour. A kiss wouldn't be enough for me this very moment. And I already told you I am not going to take advantage of you."

He brought both hands around her waist. "I don't want an adventure with you, Azzurra, I want much more," he whispered.

Her heart skipped a beat. It was so easy to agree, but she couldn't afford to start something that would have to end at one stage.

"I need to go back home," she said.

"Home could be here. You belong here."

"I do love it here, but a huge piece of my heart belongs to Australia. My life is there."

"Your life can be anywhere you want to be. Don't miss out on something incredible only because you are accustomed to some things."

"I feel torn," she whispered.

He dropped his hands from her waist. "Good night, Azzurra." He kissed her forehead and walked away.

CHAPTER 7

F amily documents and photos filled the elegant walnut cabinet. Azzurra sat on the floor of the library and went through everything. She started categorizing and labelling everything, like she would do at work. Being a librarian came in handy. In one of the boxes she noticed old photos and she started looking through them. *Mamma* Nunzia came in with a cup of hot chocolate, handed it to her, and sat on the floor next to her. Every photo, she would tell her the names of who the people were.

"*Nonno e nonna*." She pointed in a photo where the whole family was photographed.

"Why is my *nonna* next to *Zio* Vincenzo?"

Mamma tried to explain. Azzurra could understand some words that she been hearing day after day, but the rest remained gibberish to her.

"It's okay. I will ask Santo. Thank you. I feel there are a few skeletons in my family's closet."

She remembered the stranger who lived on the opposite side of the church. One night, as Azzurra walked back to the villa, she came out of her house, hugged Azzurra tightly, and then went back inside. At that time she thought it had been some crazy Italian tradition, but now that she thought about it, she looked a bit like her *nonna* Filippa.

She took the photo and got up. After putting on her heavy coat, she made her way down towards the village. Though it was cold, she saw many women outside their doors chatting. The original Facebook chatting and sharing, she laughed.

"*Buongiorno*." She saluted everyone.

Everyone smiled and answered, "*Buongiorno, Signorina Beamondo*." Some would mention a coffee, but she wasn't sure what they would say, maybe invite her in? But she kept going on her mission.

She stopped at the door where she'd seen that old woman rush in, knocked, and waited for someone to answer. The same old woman opened the door. Looking at her closer, she was a copy of her own *nonna*. She knew she wouldn't understand her, but she needed answers.

Showing the photo and pointing at her *nonna,* she said, "This is my *nonna,* Filippa, you have to be connected with her."

The older woman took the photo and, holding it tight to her heart, started rambling words in Italian as tears streamed down her face. She took Azzurra by the hand and brought her inside her modest home. The first room was her kitchen. An open fireplace in one corner, a terracotta pot on top of the fire. On the other side sat a small Christmas tree with a very small nativity set under it. The place smelled delicious even though she didn't know what she was cooking. A small wooden table stood in the middle of the room surrounded by a few chairs. On one side, a white sink with pots and pans hung from the wall, and on the other side a cupboard. She showed her a chair at the table to sit, and went to get something from the top drawer of her credenza.

She came back with photos and a necklace. One of the photos had three little girls. She pointed at one of the girls and she said, "Filippa." Then she pointed at the older girl and said, "Rosa." She said pointing the last girl, "*Io, Zia* Giovanna."

Between the sign language and the bit of Italian Azzurra had learned the past weeks, she understood the woman said, "Me, Aunty Giovanna."

She probably didn't even know that her sister was dead, and she had no way of telling her. She watched as she started making coffee and brought out some delicious biscuits. Suddenly, the door opened and three women entered. The same women who had come to visit her at the villa.

They greeted her and then helped themselves to the sweets on the table and started chatting to *Zia* Giovanna. The whole scene made Azzurra feel comfortable. There were no pretences with the people of this village, and they were who they were.

Her great aunty sat next to her, and she held her hands. She wanted to tell her about her grandmother. She had no way of communicating though. She would have to come back with Santo another time.

A knock come at the door, and a young man made his way in. "We never met before, but I am Alfredo, Giovanna's grandson."

"You speak English, thank God. How come I never met you before?"

"I study in the University of Messina in Sicily. I am back on my school holidays."

He looked about her age. Dark hair, brown eyes, and tall. A good looking boy. She wasn't sure what was in the water of Messignadi, but the whole young population was good looking.

"I heard down at the pub that you come to visit my *nonna,* and I wanted to come and say hi."

"I'm so glad you did. I don't understand anything that she is trying to say to me."

She could see his grandmother talking to him, for sure telling him to ask many questions.

"*Nonna* wants to know how her sister is doing."

"Here the most difficult question has arrived," she said. "I have no nice ways to give this information out, but my grandmother passed away a long time ago."

She waited for him to translate. The older woman started crying, and she felt for her. Tears crept down Azzurra's face as well. She hugged the old woman.

"Please tell her, she had a happy life. I remember her always smiling and telling jokes."

While Alfredo repeated her words, the old aunty smiled.

"She said it sounded like her sister, since at a very young age she was always full of life."

After a while Azzurra got up. "*Zia* Giovanna, I have to go."

"I hope I will see you soon," said Alfredo.

"I expect you to come and visit me anytime at the villa."

"I promise I will."

Once that was established, she said good bye to everyone, the older woman hugged her, and off she went.

CHAPTER 8

*A*ny girl would own at least one little black dress, and she loved all of hers, but apparently in Messignadi black was for funerals, not weddings. Not wanting to upset anyone, Azzurra chose a pale pink dress that she had brought from Australia.

With Santo, they went to the bride's house. The place appeared very modest. They waited in the dining room. Many guests were already there, as custom required. They all enjoyed a glass of liquor, or something stronger for men, and a sweet.

"It's time for you, *Signorina* Azzurra," the bride's mother said as she popped her head inside the room. "Follow me into the main bedroom."

While all this happened, Santo interpreted for her.

"Time for what?" she asked Santo.

"For you to put the veil on the bride."

"Oh God, I forgot about that."

"It's a huge honor for them. It's been many years since we had a lady from your family."

"But I am no one special."

"You are here in Messignadi."

According to tradition, the lady of the Beamondo family would veil the bride. Azzurra tried to lock in all the information Santo gave her.

"What about my great uncle? What was his role?"

"He would throw money in the streets of the village walking behind the bride." He paused, then continued, "Now I will be doing that as respect."

She entered the bedroom where the bride sat in front of the vanity, ready and waiting. The modest and small bedroom smelled sweet. A tray with sweets and small glasses filled with liquors sat on the vanity. A few women dressed elegantly smiling at her. The intimate family members. She was learning quickly.

"You look absolutely beautiful Isabella." She took her extended hands and squeezed them. "I wish you a happy life."

"I am so happy that you came, Azzurra. I will be the most envied bride in Messignadi."

"You will be because your dress is stunning. You look like a princess." She gave the bride a hug.

"That's not what I meant." Isabella laughed.

"I know." She knelt down and took an envelope from her purse. "This is for you, from me. I want to thank you for inviting me to your wedding."

The bride opened the envelope, and read the card. "You tried to write this in Italian."

"I had *Zia* and *Mamma* helping me." They both giggled. "*Oh Madonna bella mia!*'

Azzurra kept on smiling at Isabella, she could see that she liked the wedding gift.

"This is too much."

"You didn't tell me if you liked it though." She kept her voice teasing. She could see from the facial expression that Isabella loved the present.

"Who wouldn't like a present like this?"

Curious faces watched them around the room. No one understood what they were saying. No one needed to know.

"I heard that you and Matteo had plans to travel the world, but you had to postpone them and were not going on a honeymoon."

"I didn't mind, I've never been anywhere anyway."

"Well, since you both work for my family business, I can make the decision to give you both time off."

When she heard from *Zia* Cata that they had a passport ready, but nowhere to go since they were both from a very modest family, Azzurra spoke to Santo about her idea. Who wouldn't want to go and see the koalas and kangaroos down under? She then spoke with Frank and Caterina, who were excited at the idea of having the young couple there.

"I must tell Matteo," she whispered.

"He knows. *Il Dottore* spoke with him about a week ago. Your mother packed your suitcase."

She was given the bridal veil, and with delicacy, she attached the sewn comb to Isabella's hair. The bride's mother passed the small glasses with a yellow liquor to toast the bride. The photographer took what seemed like a hundred photos of them, and then the father come into the bedroom to offer his arm to his daughter to walk her to the church.

While walking, Azzurra watched Santo and the father of the bride throwing silver money from their pockets in the air. The children ran around grabbing the money. A few almost tipping the bride over in their rush to collect.

Finally, they reached the steps of the church where the groom stood waiting. *How weird that the groom wasn't waiting inside the church*.

She watched, fascinated by the difference in traditions between Calabria and Australia. Two young girls held a white ribbon, a man was near one of the girls holding a pair of scissors. Then the bride climbed the few steps to the church, the groom there waiting for his bride, once they stood opposite each other he kissed her forehead. The scissors were then handed to them for the ribbon to be cut. The music started with the Ave O Maria and they made their way inside the church to get married.

This ended up being the longest ceremony she ever been too. It felt like one of those televised masses from the Vatican including a choir.

On the way out from the church, some rice and almond lollies accompanied the money thrown in the air.

"*Evviva gli sposi.*" To the bride and groom.

❧

*T*he reception took place at a villa called *Tonnara* that looked amazing on the outside. Gray stones, black windows. Almost a gothic feeling. Like every other place she'd seen so far, Christmas decorations adorned everything in sight. She moved a few steps right and the Adriatic Sea was staring at her.

"Oh my God, it's breathtaking." Before Santo could lock the car, she made her way towards the water. She took her high heels off and through the stockings she felt the coarse sand. Nothing like back home.

A row of pebbles of many sizes divided the waters from the sand. She stood there enjoying the salty air in her lungs.

"It's too cold, Azzurra, we should go inside."

"But it's so beautiful here. I want to enjoy each moment," she said, inhaling the cold wind with the salty air.

"I will bring you back. I promise."

She believed him.

They entered the reception and watched the bride and groom make their entrance as husband and wife. She loved how everyone could choose where to sit. The long table was set under the sea view, loaded with every cold cut that she could think of. Not to mention the seafood. Azzurra's mouth watered. The seven-tier buttercream wedding cake positioned in the middle of the table dominated the setting. Each tier had a different detailed pattern. White and pink orchids and lilies highlighted the top tier.

The band started playing as soon as the bride and groom had their antipasto served. People were too busy chatting and eating. Not her, she was busy tapping her foot under the table.

"When are the bride and groom going to start the dancing?"

"They won't. Or at least women won't be dancing. At the end the men will dance the folk *tarantella*."

Azzurra nodded her head. How could anyone go to a wedding and not dance?

"Are we going to dance?" she asked him.

"It might not be a good idea," said Santo.

"Maybe, but as I am from another country, I'm sure they will understand. Who knows, we might start a new trend in Messignadi."

Santo got up. "Would you do me the honor to dance with me Signorina Beamondo?"

Any excuse to be closer to him pleased her, and the idea of breaking traditions and dancing sent a thrill of excitement through her.

"I would love to dance with you, *Dottore*."

A slow ballad started them off. One hand slipped into his, and his other rested on her back. The scent of his aftershave drove her crazy. Azzurra wasn't going to deny she wanted him.

The moment he brought her closer to him, she felt his hard on. He wanted her as much as she wanted him. Azzurra was sure of that.

For a split second, she forgot the room full of people. With her hand on his neck, she pulled his face closer to her. For a moment, his face hovered near hers, and her heart leapt at the thought he might kiss her.

His lips were about to touch hers. The music stopped. Reality hit home. The guests clapped.

He brought her back to their seat.

"Thank you," he said, his voice coarse.

"You owe me," she responded, her voice matter of fact.

"Owe you what?" Santo looked unsure of what she was referring too.

"That kiss that you almost gave me in the dance floor."

"Touché," he said, smiling. Looking at her closely, he started sipping his wine.

CHAPTER 9

*B*ells ringing, pipes playing, accompanied by tambourines and singing. She reached for her iPhone and checked the time. "Oh God, it's only five am!" She wanted to go back to sleep, but she was told the *novena* would be starting this morning. Every sixteenth of December, and for nine consecutive mornings after, the town would be woken by the musicians in time for everyone to be in church by six am. The ritual was to celebrate the coming of Christmas. At least she could sleep in on the tenth morning, as it would be Christmas day.

Like a zombie, with stiff legs and making guttural moans she walked to the shower. She applied the three minutes rule, dressed, and walked downstairs.

"Good morning, sunshine." Santo sat at the table, a smug look on his face, sipping his coffee.

"I can't believe I am doing this." As she sat, *Zia* Cata brought her coffee, with her *latte and biscotti*. She got used to the Calabrese breakfast warm milk and homemade biscuits. Sometimes they would substitute the biscuits with homemade pasta dura bread.

"Well, they do say misery loves company. Thank you for making mine a bit more fun."

She definitely wasn't a morning person. She reached for his cup half full, grabbed it, and drank it.

"How about bite my ass, *Dottore*?"

He just laughed.

"Now that's a very tempting thought." They both laughed.

*T*he whole of Messignadi filled the church. It looked like the villagers took this Christmas *novena* very seriously. She could feel all eyes on her, and every time she locked eyes with someone, she would receive the biggest smile. Many children went to sit with her. By now, everyone knew about the party she planned to give them a few days before Christmas. The younger children were pushing each other to be the one to sit next to her. They even managed to push Santo out of his seat.

The youngest one waited for Azzurra to pick her up. She made herself comfortable on her lap.

The ritual had been the prayers and the singing. All the Christmas songs, with the only difference they were sang in Italian. Once it ended, the parents came to collect their children, each one saying hello to Azzurra and speaking to her, with Santo translating.

"Doesn't the rule 'never speak to strangers' apply in Messignadi?" she asked Santo, smiling.

"You are not a stranger, and children are very intuitive. They like you."

"Azzurra, it was a pleasure having you here this morning, and the children are very taken with you." The priest came once everyone left.

"I was pleasantly surprised," she said matter of fact.

"The villagers are very pleased that Don Giacomo's legacy is keeping going."

"Don Libero, is your offer still valid to take me shopping for the children's presents?"

"Of course it is. We can do either tomorrow or the day after. You will have enough time to get organized."

"I have a lot of help. My cousin Alfredo and his friends volunteered."

She had so much to organise, and not much time at all.

CHAPTER 10

"*H*ere you are." He found her. No big surprise there. She spent most of her time in the villa's library reading. His sexy smile was a fabulous break.

"I found this amazing novel from the past centuries and it's in English."

He took the book from her and read the title. "Manzoni, the father of all Italians writers."

"You read it!" It wasn't a question.

"You might need to stop your reading. You have a visitor."

"Who?"

"Your grandmother's sister, Giovanna."

Placing the book on the sofa, she got up. "My grandmother was sweet, looks like a family trait."

"It's been over fifty years since a Crispino, your grandmother's family set foot in the Beamondo property."

"I am almost too scared to ask why that is."

"Come, you want to make her feel comfortable."

She entered the room and the three ladies were in deep conversation, their faces so serious.

"*Ciao, Zia Giovanna.*" She went to the older woman and gave her a kiss on her check.

The older woman placed her hands on Azzurra's face. "*Che Dio ti benedice, nipote mia.*"

Pride filled her at how rapidly she'd started understanding simple phrases. Her great aunty had just told her, "God bless you, my niece." "Come, *vieni,*" said the older woman. A cane basket full of homemade biscuits waited on the coffee table.

"Oh my, they look delicious. Thank you. *Grazie, Zia* Giovanna."

Pointing at each different sweet, the older woman told her the names. "*Nacalote, pittopie, nzudi e stomatico.*"

"They all look amazing, so much work involved."

The face of the old aunty conveyed her happiness that Azzurra loved the present.

"If you like, I can teach you how to make them."

"Yes, I would love that very much, thank you."

For someone who never learned to cook, she found herself learning from Caterina, and now in Messignadi everyone seemed very eager to teach her different things. What she loved about the village was the afternoon siesta, but unlike the normal siesta where people would sleep, in Messignadi people would go visiting each other. Santo would come back home and be her personal interpreter on perfect afternoons.

Never the kind to tiptoe around something on her mind, Azzurra went straight to the questions. "Santo, can you ask my aunty why in the photo my grandmother was next to Zio Vincenzo instead of my grandfather?"

She hadn't asked Santo, or his mum and aunty, as she wanted to know from someone who was there at the time.

"Apparently Filippa had been promised to Don Vincenzo as a bride. But the night before the wedding took place, Rosario and Filippa ran away together and never kept in contact with anyone."

"They fell in love," she whispered.

"In a small village what they did was the ultimate betrayal."

"Now it's clear why they became Ross and Phyllis and never looked back." While she felt sorry for the dead great-uncle, at least her grandparents had been a couple in love. So much in love, in fact, that they left everything behind.

Though the bell remained a sore subject between her and Santo, she wanted to know more.

Zia Giovanna started telling Santo in Calabrese all about it. The huge earthquake of the 5th of April 1783. The pride of the village, the convent, had been destroyed. It happened the day the village celebrates Saint Vincent Ferreri. Instead, they lost not only houses, but almost three hundred inhabitants. From the convent, the only thing that had been saved was the small bell called the Younger Sister, and the big statue of Saint Vincent that is now in the village church.

"What about the other bell?" she asked.

Zia Giovanna, the oldest there, started telling her about how they never found it, but some people could still hear the bell ringing.

"Is it just a legend, you think?" Azzurra asked.

"If you want to believe in something, you don't have to see it. You just put your faith in it," said the older woman.

"How do you feel if I want to bring back the bell next to the other?"

Her great aunty got up, gave her a kiss on her forehead and said, "Be careful who you trust. Not everyone who comes in your path will have good intentions." She posed one hand on Azzurra's heart and continued. "Follow your heart. If it tells you to do it then listen, but first hear everything else around you." The conversation took place entirely in Calabrese, and Santo translated word for word.

To Azzurra, it felt like she had given the blessing, but in the same breath was cautioning her to let the thing be. She was more confused than ever.

She then wanted to know about her family, the generations before her. As the stories were told, she felt more proud with every moment to be part of the Beamondo family. They had been the Landlords of Messignadi for many generations. Half of the families of the village were working for her. She knew the day would come that she would have to go back to Australia, but while she lived in Calabria, she would make sure to look after everyone. She learned many things about her family this day, and since she came to Messignadi she had learned many things about Santo.

It was common knowledge that Santo would help anyone who went to him, not just as a doctor. If they had a problem they would go to him. He would give them money if they were in need of it. Buy books and stationary for those kids who the parents couldn't afford it. She knew he was a good man, a man she trusted, a man she found attractive, but a man she would have to leave behind once she would go back home.

Once the old aunty left, Azzurra followed Santo in his office.

"Interesting facts." She replayed everything in her mind, absorbing all the details in fascination.

"You have a rich family history, you should be very proud."

"I am. I listened to everything," she said.

"Still decided to dig the big bell out?" he asked.

She stepped closer, looking straight into his big brown eyes. "I know you don't agree."

He stood there silently.

"I need to research more about this. One thing is sure, I will never sell my land to those men."

"Finally, we agree on something."

"Once I'm gone, you'll have the freedom to make any decision. You care about the villagers and their wellbeing."

"You might not feel it yet, but you do belong here."

"I've never been brought up to think I was Italian."

She always felt her grandparents were running from something. She was the only one with no family on her father's side. Her mother's Irish heritage remained another story altogether. Azzurra and her family always lived among English speaking people in far north Queensland. She never had contact with anyone of Italian background. After high school and her librarian qualifications, she moved in the city where she met Frank and Catarina, her Italian neighbours. They often said she was their adopted daughter.

"When I received the letter from the mayor, I didn't want to come. I had no interest in coming here. I definitely didn't want anything. I wanted to send a letter back and say, 'keep everything, I'm washing my hands,' but Frank insisted that I should come and be in touch with my roots." Extending her arms, she said, "Here I am in this strange little village full of history. When I touched those bricks in the convent, the furniture in the villa, I felt the history in my veins. Don't get me wrong, I love my country and will always be an Australian, but I'm also starting to feel things for this place that I never thought possible."

"This is the land of your grandparents, and though your mother was Irish, you have also their blood in your veins," said Santo.

Life was unpredictable. While some would live in joy and happiness, others would be left in pain. Like old great-uncle Vincenzo had been.

"I should let you work. Your faithful patients will start to come soon."

She'd spent long enough here to learn the villager's habits.

*B*efore she could go, Santo went closer and placed his lips on hers. For a moment the world felt still. She closed her eyes and enjoyed the sweet kiss.

68

CHAPTER 11

*A*zzurra decided to go shopping in the commercial center in a bigger village nearby with Father Libero. She was happy to see that her cousin had also come with his friend and his van, big enough to bring the toys back to the villa.

They helped choose the right toys. For the under three years old, they bought many stuffed bears. The older ones, the theme was cars for the boys and dolls for the girls. The shop assistant seemed unable to believe her eyes when they went to pay. For a moment neither could Azzurra. The total amount equated two months of her salary back home.

"I can't wait to see the children's faces once they get the presents," she said.

"It will be an eventful day," the priest said, smiling.

The two young men took most of the toys in the van. "We meet you at the villa." With that they went.

Father Libero went to get his car while Azzurra waited near the door.

She could hear footfalls behind her. She turned around and

she saw Nandini, one of the men she'd met in the mayor's office.

"Well, well, well, *Signorina* Beamondo. What a surprise to see you so far from your villa."

"Now that is something completely stupid to say. Why is that a surprise?"

"Settle down, no need to be defensive. I thought I would come and say hello."

She didn't trust him the other day, and sure as hell she didn't trust him now.

"Maybe today, now that you are away from your watch dog, we can have a serious chat about your decision."

"*Dottore De Angelis* is no one's watch dog," she said, fed up with his passive aggressive behavior.

"Glad to hear that. So let me just say. If you decide to sell us the land, we can make you a very rich woman. In effect, you can name your price."

How these people couldn't take no for an answer scared her. "We already spoke about this, and I gave you all my answer in the mayor's office."

"I don't feel that our conversation was over. I think we still have a lot of things to talk about."

"I don't usually change my mind on things. I don't think anything you have to say will change my mind."

"Do you understand how big an opportunity it is for everyone involved?"

"I am not money hungry. I don't really care about money. I think Messignadi needs love, needs caring. I don't think they need another road for the train." She paused for a moment. "Not many travel at all, and the ones that do have cars."

"I see you are as stubborn as your uncle was."

Before Azzurra could answer, she heard Father Libero. "What's going on here? Is this man harassing you?" he asked.

"No one is harassing anyone," the man answered in a defensive tone.

"Hey Father, nothing I can't handle don't worry."

"*Signorina*, before you go, I wanted to mention...have you any idea how many people had to emigrate up to north Italy, Germany, even in Australia so they can feed their families? If you could see the future the way I can, you would see how many job opportunities would be available for the people of your village."

"They would have a job while they work on the railway yes, and then? I will not be responsible for destroying thousands of years old olive trees and sending those same people away from their land to find jobs once they have nothing to do back home to survive."

"Your uncle was too old to see the future, but you? You are a woman of the modern society and still you don't want to see progress in your own village."

"Enough!" yelled the priest. "She gave you the answer in so many forms. Now leave the girl alone and find another project to fill your time in the council."

No answer back to that. One thing Azzurra had learned, in small Italian villages priests had more power than politicians.

❦

*S*anto had been away at the capital city. One of his patients had an appointment to see a specialist, and he wanted to be there with him. She really loved how he cared for everyone. He was a humanitarian, even if he didn't see it that way.

She went upstairs, knocked at Santo's door, and received no answer. She opened the door to see if he maybe had fallen asleep.

He stood near his wardrobe, his hands on each door, looking for what to wear most likely. His nude male figure stood straight and proud. She was about to back step her way out when he turned around. They looked at each other, for a moment neither spoke or moved. Azzurra broke their gaze and concentrated on the rest of him. Without any shame, she enjoyed the vision in front of her. Tall, strong, and proud. Her eyes stopped on his crotch. Within moments an erection stared at her.

"I should put some pants on."

They gazed at one another.

"If you really must."

He shook his head and while smiling, reached for his jeans and put them on.

"No undies?" she asked.

"It was a quick reaction, I suppose," he answered.

Azzurra sat on his bed and looked at him. "It's quite erotic knowing you have no undies on."

"Are we about to play with fire?"

"No!" Spell broken again "I need to tell you what happened today when I went shopping with Father Libero."

"I have a better idea," he said.

"You don't want to know?"

"You can tell me all about it in the car."

"Where are we going?"

"I was going to come and tell you in the kitchen. I'm taking you to Villa San Giovanni for my kind of dancing."

"Sounds like a perfect plan." She got up from the bed and walked towards the door.

"What should I wear?" she asked.

"I want to be the most envied man there tonight. Wear your prettiest dress. Villa is the prettiest city in Calabria."

"Sounds like a good plan. What's the name of the nightclub?"

"We are not going to a nightclub. The dancing is in the

Piazza, near the waters, and the old castle and the most marvellous view of Sicily on the other side of the waters."

"It sounds kind of magical."

Santo walked to her, and grabbed one of her hands into his. He placed the other on her hip, bringing her closer to him. A tremor went through Azzurra's body. Having him this close made her weak at her knees.

"Dancing the liscio is like making love," he said softly.

"I better go and get ready then, *Dottore*." She gave him a soft kiss on his lips and she went.

Azzurra chose carefully what to wear for this very special night. It was almost Christmas and she wanted to wear sparkles. The black dress she chose brushed her knees, no sleeves, with a velvet sash that crossed under her breast and coming down on her hips. Sheer material on her waist and sparkles everywhere else. She chose her high heels, black and shiny with open toe. She pulled her hair in a high bun, the only decoration a pair of long black and silver earring, with a bracelet and a ring to match.

She applied light foundation to her entire face, accompanied by a sheer highlighter on her cheekbones. For her cheeks she decided on a peach blush.

For her eyes, she decided to go for a classic smoky cat eyes, with a rich purple and a grey accompanied by eyeliner and mascara. A neutral beige lip-gloss and she was ready.

She looked at herself in the mirror, and smiled approval. "Ok, girl, let's go and get your man."

He waited in the lounge for her, dressed in a navy blue suit, white shirt, and camel tie. And the best smile to match. "You look stunning," Santo said the moment he laid eyes on her.

Before she could say anything, *Mamma* Nunzia came next to her.

"*Non puoi uscire cosi, fa freddo e ti ammali.*" *You can't go out like that, it's cold and you will get sick.*

After over a month living in Messignadi, Azzurra got used to the typical Italian mother. She gave the older woman a hug and a kiss on her check. "Stop worrying, *Mamma*, I have my coat and am going from the door to the car."

Before they could go, *Zia* Cata came into the room to say goodbye.

"Are they behind the curtain?" Azzurra asked as she put the seat belt on in the car.

"Just wave goodbye; that will make them happy."

"I have a feeling that they are match making us."

Santo laughed, then said. "You are not wrong there. *Mamma* wants grandchildren, and the sooner I marry, the sooner she will become a *nonna*."

"You have to marry to be a father?"

"Azzurra this is Messignadi, not Australia."

She let out a laugh. "I think I have learned the ways of the village. I was teasing you. When was your last meaningful relationship?"

"About ten years ago. But it didn't work out."

"What went wrong?"

"She assumed that I was Don Vincenzo's son. She lived in a village nearby. When I told her the truth, her family didn't think I was good enough to marry her."

"It doesn't make sense."

"In small villages, most girls do what their family wants. I suppose she wasn't in love with me as much as I was with her."

"It must have been hard for you."

"I was heartbroken. After my degree, your uncle sent me to England, hoping that my heart would mend and that I would learn English." He smiled at her. "Life goes on and what was important once is not anymore."

"Time heals many things."

"What about you? Have you ever been in love?"

"Yes, I was stupidly in love. I met him at the time I lost my parents. He was charming, I was so ready to settle. Then he betrayed me." She stopped for a moment, then continued. "I had a housemate, I thought she was a nice girl, until she ran away with my boyfriend, leaving me three months of rent to pay."

"How did you resolve your financial situation?"

"Frank and Caterina helped me. They became my surrogate parents, you can say."

"I believe that when a woman who suffered is loved correctly, she becomes ten times more the woman she was before." He grabbed her hand and held it tight. "I'm sorry for all you went through, but don't give up on love. Not everyone is like your ex, or like my ex. We need to believe in that."

"I really want to believe in that. I want to experience that feeling of fuzziness in the pit of my belly again. I want to feel safe, to be loved."

"You will get there, I promise you."

They arrived at a huge Piazza. He parked the car in the carpark and they walked towards the restaurant. The Christmas lights were a serious business. They looked gorgeous and in the middle the biggest Christmas tree she ever saw rose majestically. The waters of the sea were like a huge black pearl, and the cold breeze wasn't as bad as she first thought.

A band was already playing, and people filled the tables, dining and listening to the music. A kerosene heater sat next to each table, keeping the patrons warm.

"If you prefer, we can sit inside," Said Santo.

"No, I want to experience this."

"*Cameriere,* I have a booking for two. The name is De Angelis."

"Of course, *Dottore*, you would prefer to sit inside or under the stars?"

"Out here is fine, maybe that table there near the wall so it won't be too cold for the *Signorina*."

"Of course, *Dottore*, please follow me."

Santo held the chair for her. Azzurra sat and looked around. The incredible panorama took her breath away. Darkness and little lights spread out all over the other side of the waters.

"How did the waiter know you're a doctor?" she asked.

"I do come often with my colleagues for work meetings."

"That's Sicily, and the highest light is the Mount Etna," said Santo.

"It's absolutely gorgeous."

"At the moment Etna is asleep, but a few months ago, it gave the Sicilians a bit of a scare."

The waiter brought the menus. Of course they were all in Italian.

"Can you please order for me?" She smiled.

"Of course, I know nothing with chilli."

The wine had been a sweet homemade, and their dishes were all fish based. Local dishes of course.

"Oh my god, this is magical, like a film."

"Would you like to dance?" asked Santo.

"I would love too."

It had been years since she danced the tango. Her grandad would dance with her every Saturday night at the RSL club when she was a child. Their bodies close, one hand into his, the other on his shoulder. The vibrant music started. Azzurra was happy to follow Santo's lead, maintaining the harmony of the music and connecting through the embrace.

"Nothing else exists in this very moment," he whispered. "We can forget about the reality and let the music take over."

"It's truly magic," she said, not breaking their gaze.

Lips met, the kiss soft and delicate.

She felt safe in his arms. Every step they took was subsequently beautiful. The music seemed like a kiss on her skin. Each pore vibrated by the beat and the touch of Santo.

The music took a break. He brought her back to their table, kissed her hand, held her chair, and she sat.

"I'm glad I didn't step on your toes. It's been years since I danced the tango."

"It's like riding a bike, you never forget."

"I used to dance with my grandad at the club on Saturday night."

"I must confess, I am glad dancing the tango didn't make you think of an ex-boyfriend."

"My ex wasn't the romantic type. So everything I've been doing with you is not taking me back in time." She laughed.

He reached for her and caressed his thumb across her lower lip. "It's a very nice feeling when I'm next to you. I feel alive again. I don't want to scare you away."

At that she shook her head, smiling. "You're not. I won't lie, all this is new to me." She grabbed his hand and gave a small kiss on the back of it.

He smiled.

"It really feels so good being in your arms. I feel like a princess."

"You are a princess for the right man."

"If it's a dream, I don't want to wake up."

"No, it's not a dream. It's all real. Maybe we need to seriously see where this could take us. We both are trying to push each other away for fear of getting hurt again, but this could be a step towards believing in love again." he said.

"I need to go back home." She couldn't stop the sadness that laced her voice.

"Don't they say home is where the heart is?" He looked at her intensely. "I can't tell you what to do. I can't ask you to stay if your heart feels you have to go back to Australia. I can only say open your heart and live this moment. We won't have another chance at this once you are gone. I don't want to live a life with regrets."

"It would be so easy to let myself go. Forget about everything and just live this moment with you." She let go of his hand. She took a sip of her wine, it wasn't enjoyable as it grew tasteless in her mouth. "I miss home. I'm not sure I belong here."

"It's normal to miss home. I'm not asking to turn your back on who you are. Just give this a chance."

She had mixed feelings. She wanted to be in his arms, but feared what tomorrow would bring.

"Just let's live this moment. Let's not worry about what tomorrow will bring."

"What if one of us will get hurt?" She let out a sigh, then continued. "I want to believe in the magic, but I've never had the luxury to dream."

"Please don't think of the painful past. We both had painful experiences. Let's feel this moment between you and I. Let's pretend nothing else exists."

It had been years since she felt the butterflies in her stomach. She wasn't a woman to fall in love easily. But after a month of spending every day with him, it awoke feelings inside that she thought forever buried.

"Are you ready to go home?" he asked.

She nodded. He paid the bill and went to get the car. Neither spoke on the way home. Each sat quietly with their own thoughts, but still holding hands.

"We are home, Azzurra." He got out of the car, opened her door, and hand in hand they walked inside the villa. He helped her take off her coat, then he took off his and hung them both on the rack in the entrance.

In silence, they made their way upstairs until they stopped at her door. He took one hand and slowly raised to his lips and kissed it.

"Thank you for tonight." His voice sounded coarse.

She opened the door, and he stepped closer, grabbing her by

her hips and giving her a passionate kiss. She walked backwards while kissing him back. No words were needed.

She broke the kiss and turned around to look at the bed. He encircled his arms around her and started kissing her neck.

"You want me to go?" he asked, still holding her tight.

She wiggled her way around to face him, circled her arms around his neck, and shook her head. Fear and a knot of emotion froze her throat. If she tried to voice her thoughts, she might cry.

They say the woman always decides when to sleep with a man. For that they would wear their best underwear. Tonight she did just that, not knowing that the night would end up with Santo in her room.

They walked to the bed, and while kissing, Santo unzipped her black dress, peeling it off her body. She stepped out of it.

She stood there in her French black knickers and bra that matched and watched Santo taking off his jacket, then his tie.

Santo brought her closer, his lips on her neck again. His hands ran all along her arms and back.

"I dreamed of this moment since I laid eyes on you," he whispered. One arm wrapped around her waist, just above her buttocks. The other arm circled around her shoulder, enveloping her in a gentle embrace. He bent down to find her lips with a soft touch. It was a hungry kiss, and she matched his hunger. She raised her arms to his neck and massaged his hair.

"I really love kissing you," she said once their kiss broke. She raised her head and smiled at him. Slowly, she started unbuttoning his shirt. One button at the time. Once the shirt came off his shoulders, Azzurra stared at his firm chest for a few moments, then slowly she started caressing every inch.

He stopped her hands. "You are driving me crazy."

Slowly, they both lay on the bed, kissing and stripping the remaining clothing off each other. She tried to undo his belt, but it was stuck. With one hand he helped her, then took his pants off, the boxers next. She could feel his arousal on her hip.

She didn't want to ruin the moment, but safety remained important to her. Always had been.

"We need protection," she whispered while he kissed her neck. When he stopped, Azzurra wasn't sure how he had taken that. Her mind went to millions of ways in only a moment. "I am always very careful." She waited.

"I wouldn't want you any other way." His answer gave Azzurra the understanding that she needed.

She took the condoms from the side cabinet and she put them under the pillow, then, returned to kissing him.

"Tell me to stop." His head rose, looking at her.

She smiled, moving like a happy feline. "I don't think so."

With a quick movement, he unclipped her bra. His hands then on her hips, he peeled off her stockings, then her knickers, flinging them somewhere on the floor. With his hands, he caressed her whole body, from her neck, to her firm breasts, stomach and round hips, moving to her inner thighs around to her buttocks.

He placed his lips where his hands had been moments before, until he reached her inner thighs. He opened her legs and went straight to the middle where her pussy was. His tongue found her clitoris.

"Oh God." That's all she could say as his mouth found her pussy again. He gently grasped one breast, as he kept his hand there, making his grip stronger while he moved his head between her thighs. His tongue caressed against her clit, taking her to scintillating pleasure. It had been so long since Azzurra experienced the flutter at the touch of a man, and Santo played the perfect role of partner. She nearly protested when he sat back up and the pleasure receded. A pearl of pre-cum decorated his tip, and she leaned forward, eager to taste him. His firm but gentle hand on her shoulder stopped her.

"Not tonight, darling. Tonight is all about you," he said, his voice thick with need.

She smiled. Though she wanted to return the favor, she also wanted him to take the lead.

Between kisses, she felt his hand under the pillow. He removed one from the strip, and the air around them echoed with the sound of him ripping it open. At that, Azzurra plucked the rubber from his fingers. Participation from the sidelines didn't suit her. She preferred the hands-on approach. She revelled in the hardness of his cock as she rolled the condom down the length of him "How would you like it?" he asked.

"I haven't prayed in a while. I suppose missionary is the right way to start." Their joint laughter set her at ease and solidified her desire to be with him. Santo's eyes hardened with lust once more as he settled between her thighs, resting his tip at her entrance. With a thrust, he penetrated her, and a gasp of pleasure escaped her lips.

"I feel blessed," he joked back.

Within seconds, they found the perfect rhythm. Coming with Santo proved easy for Azzurra. Time and time again. With each climax, Azzurra let out a scream.

"This is heaven," he said between breaths. Suddenly he grabbed her by her hips and made her stop. "I am not ready to end this yet," he said. They kept on kissing again until she trembled underneath him. Moving onto his knees, he grabbed one of her legs and rested it on his shoulder. He started kissing her feet, making his way up to her upper leg. His hard cock rocked inside of her.

While moaning in pleasure, she grabbed the sheets with one hand brought the other to his head.

Lowering her leg back, he positioned himself closer and started kissing her. Azzurra reached for his cock and took control of it, helping him slide all the way in. The moment he penetrated her, they gazed into each other's eyes before sharing an intimate kiss.

"This is heaven," she whispered as the kiss broke.

He then started his rhythm, following the pace of her undulating hips. At first slowly and deep, then more intense. They sped up until they both reached the wildest orgasm. For a moment neither moved. Then brought her into his arms.

Words were not needed. The passion that they shared had been nothing compared to the intimacy they shared after sex.

"Will you stay with me all night?" she asked.

"There is no other place I would rather be."

CHAPTER 12

*A*lmost Christmas. Only two days away. Azzurra's first white Christmas. The festivities around the village were contagious. Today marked a special day. She was going to give a Christmas party to the children of Messignadi. But before that, Santo took her around to see her workers. Each group, on a different farm. She wanted to let them know personally that she had no intention of selling the land, and that even when she went back their job remained safe.

All the ladies of the village involved themselves in preparing the food for the party, while the younger ones helped Azzurra decorate the school hall.

She went to the church to get the last items and there she met Rocco, the sacristan.

"I got the Santa suit, Rocco, are you ready?" If it wasn't for the sign language that was so universal, she was sure no one would understand her as that bit of Italian she had learned wasn't enough.

Waiting patiently for Rocco to change, Azzurra took her camera out from her backpack and started taking photos. One click after the other took her to the stairs. As she looked up she noticed the bell. The Younger Sister, as the villagers called her. She heard so many different stories of the big bell, a part of her wanted to do what Santo wanted, but the other part told her this could be good for the village.

"Would you like to go upstairs and see it?" asked Rocco, already dressed up with a big tummy and a white beard. His English sounded very broken, but enough to be understood.

"You speak English?' she asked.

"I lived in Australia for *quattro anni*. Four years," he said as he opened the small gate for her and invited her to lead the way. One hundred and fifty steps. Azzurra counted them one by one. By the time she reached the top, she was almost out of breath. She looked at the bell close up, took photos, then from the open window she looked at Messignadi. She could see the village from every angle.

"*Quella e` la tua villa.*" *That is your villa.* Rocco pointed. "On that side you can see as far as *Oppido Mamertina*. On this side you can see past the cemetery."

Azzurra took as many photos as she could. The usual terracotta colored roofs were now covered in white fluffy snow, while the Aspromonte Mountains loomed in distance with whitecaps. "Have you ever heard the big bell ring?" she asked.

"That land is sacred, and I did hear the bell ring once when my brother got killed."

"I'm sorry to hear that."

"He is in a better place." He stopped a moment. "The place of the truth and sooner or later we all shall go there."

"I hope later, much later," she said.

"I agree with you, *Signorina Azzurra*."

"Ready to go, Rocco?"

They arrived at the hall. Rocco hid in the back room where all the presents were. Kids ran around having fun, while the village band played songs. The tables were full of food. She had planned on giving the children an Australian Christmas party.

The ladies in her family, including *Zia* Giovanna, followed her instructions by making party pies, little sausage rolls, and scones with cream and jam.

Not too many people were missing from this party. Only a few that had a feud with her family a few generations ago. One thing she had learned, people could hold grudges for generations and not know why.

"Did you bring your Santa?" asked Santo.

"I sure did. He's back there waiting for his introduction."

He walked closer. She could smell the scent of his skin. "I can't stop thinking of last night, of the two of us," he whispered.

"*Dottore,* you are going to get me into trouble."

"Nah, the whole village believes we should get married anyway."

She didn't laugh, she just looked at him. "I know I've been told by many. But we both know."

"Yes, I know. You must go back to Australia."

"At this stage I'm confused."

"Tonight, your room or mine?"

"Mine. It's far from the two mother hens."

"Oh yes, we must be careful because you're a screamer."

Before she could hit him with something, Don Libero come to get her to introduce Santa. She shook her head, smiling. She knew that she was more involved that she cared to admit. Proudly she looked around. Her family had been here for generations. She was starting to fall in love not only with Santo, but with this old village and its people who were absolutely amazing.

Once Santa came into the room, the kids were buzzing with joy. Then he called one by one by their names and Azzurra helped him give out the presents.

Father Libero came running to her, trying to stop her.

"What's wrong, Father?"

"We haven't done the blessing of the toys," he said.

"Again? Father, I'm sure God will understand."

"I'm sure you're right, dear, please carry on," said the priest.

She walked to where Alfredo and the musicians were. "Thank you, guys, this wouldn't have been possible without your help."

"It was our pleasure, cuz."

They come back from the party, singing Christmas songs in the car. So far she'd had the most amazing time. Everyone made her feel at home. Her life had changed so much in the past month and a half. She took photos and a few little videos to send to Frank and Catarina. She knew they would have been so proud of her.

"Home sweet home," said Santo.

"Go in everyone, and have a good night."

While *Mamma* Nunzia and *Zia* Cata made their way to the villa, Azzurra waited in the car.

"I thought you were going to spend the night with me." She didn't want to sound disappointed, but that's how she felt.

He looked around the see if the two older women entered the villa. Once the door closed, he brought his hand to her face and gave her a kiss on her lips.

"Try keeping me away from you!' he said. "I have to finish the reports that I must send to the Policlinic in Reggio Calabria. If I send them by tomorrow, I will get the results before the New Year."

"Then you will come up?"

"Then I will be where I belong into your arms."

*S*omething woke Azzurra up. She stretched in the bed and reached for Santo. He wasn't there. She looked at her iPhone. Three am. Suddenly she heard a bell ring.

"What the hell is going on in the village?"

Quickly, she put her sweatpants and sweater on top of her silky pajamas, her dressing gown on top, and her house shoes, and made her way downstairs. She walked slowly. She didn't want to wake up anybody else. The closer she walked to the front door the louder the bell sounded.

She opened the door as the bell continued ringing. Suddenly she felt a shiver down her spine. No, it wasn't the cold weather. Was it her imagination, or was the bell the legendary sentinel that everyone spoke of in the village? She walked outside to the porch, and looked towards the clinic.

Flames came out of the clinic's window. "Oh my God! Santo." Her scream pierced the air. She tried to remember what she had learned from her fire lessons she took at work. Unfortunately, there were no fire alarms in the villa. The only thing she could do was run towards the stairs and yell as loud as she could, "Fire!"

She knew very well that going towards the fire wasn't the most intelligent action to take, but her only thought was that man she loved remained trapped in the flames. As she reached the clinic she saw Pasquale and the two women following her.

Suddenly, the bell stopped ringing. She had no time to think if it had been her imagination, but either way because of the ringing, she discovered the fire. She only hoped that it wasn't too late.

"A unde' me fighiu?" yelled *Mamma* Nunzia. *Where is my son?*

"I heard the bell ringing and I saw the fire, he must be in his office. *Nel suo ufficio*"

Other words weren't needed.

Zia Cata went to the phone, while Azzura was already off the porch and heading toward the clinic. They were following her.

She couldn't let panic take over her. She took her dressing gown off to have more freedom of movement. Then she grabbed a log and broke the window's glass. The flames were climbing towards the roof, and the smoke hung so thick that it made it impossible to see anything.

She tried to climb over the window, but Pasquale held her.

"No *Signorina*, we need you safe. I go in."

He climbed the window himself, getting lost into the greyness of the smoke.

She jumped on the windowsill, trying to see if Santo was in there, and spotted him leaning against the desk. She watched Pasquale grab him, position him on top of his shoulder, and stumble back to the window as coughs racked the air. What lasted a few minutes felt like hours to her.

She was about to grab him, but other arms come to the rescue. Half of the village men were already there, ready to help. They placed him on the ground. She touched his pulse.

"He's alive." She only hoped that it wasn't too late. She wanted to cry and scream her own pain, but she had to keep a cool head.

"Take him to his room," she said to Pasquale.

"Call the doctor from next village. He can be here in less than ten minutes."

"*Sta arrivando*," said *Zia* Cata, was there next to her. *He's on his way.* Then went to her sister who was only able to cry for her son.

A few of the men helped Pasquale take Santo inside the villa followed by *Mamma* and *Zia* crying.

Azzurra started helping the men carrying buckets of water trying to stop the fire.

She never felt this much fear in her life. As she passed the buckets of water automatically, she thought about the legend of the village's bell. She had been so sceptical, now she knew Santo had been saved by the bell.

If she didn't hear those rings, she would not have made it to alert everyone. Santo would have been dead. This was the very moment she knew she loved him. The fear of losing him made her heart skip a few beats.

She kept turning around to stare at the villa.

"*Signorina,* go inside, we have things under control in here," said Pasquale.

She dropped the bucket and ran inside.

Santo lay in the middle of the bed, and she didn't wait to be invited in. She went to him and knelt at his side.

"He inhaled a lot of smoke, but he will be fine in a couple of days."

"Thank you, Doctor, it's been an eventful night. And thank you for coming to his aid so soon."

Both *Mamma* Nunzia and *Zia* Cata knelt next to her. She hugged both women.

"*Tutto bene ora.* Everything is good now," she said.

Santo started coughing. Azzurra let his mom and aunty go to him. She got up and moved back a few steps.

"Azzurra." His voice sounded deep and faint.

"*Andiamo tutti fuori.* Everyone, let's go outside," said his mother, while pulling Azzurra by her hand closer to the bed.

She sat at the edge of the bed, leaned closer to him, and speaking softly in a voice that bordered on a whisper, said, "I am here, Santo."

"You are so beautiful," he said between gasps.

"Please don't talk now, try resting. I will stay with you."

He shook his head. "I need to say something."

"Please rest, the investigation will be done and we will find out who's the culprit here."

"No, I wanted to say that I love you."

Tears started trailing down her cheeks. She'd feared that he'd died and she would never have the chance to tell him how she felt.

"I love you too, Santo."

"Will you stay with me?" he asked.

"I won't leave your side, and I am sure we can work out the rest."

"I am sure we will."

She went closer and kissed his lips.

"Thank you for saving me," he whispered. "Pasquale told the doctor you alerted everyone."

"Santo De Angelis, you have been saved by the bell."

"You heard it ring?"

She nodded her head, smiling. "The legend has become our reality. You were right. Messignadi needs the bell as their sentinel. It belongs underground."

"Same as you need to be where you belong, in my arms."

Now wasn't the time to kiss him passionately, he needed all the air that he could get. They had a life time of kisses and loving each other.

Recipes are for the first meal Azzurra ate in Messignadi. They are from the book *Pane, Vino E PEPERONCINO; Flavors of Calabria* www.giusycaporetto.com

RAGÙ SAUCE

Ingredients:
500 grams of pork
1 kilo of crushed tomatoes
Basil
1 glass of red wine
1 onion
Oil
Salt and pepper

Method for preparation:
Heat the oil in a saucepan, add the meat and the onions and stir until they reach a golden brown colour.

Add the wine, salt and pepper.

When the wine is completely dry, add the tomatoes.

Bring to boiling over high heat and add the basil, then lower the heat and cook for 3 hours, adding a little water from time to time.

MEATBALLS

Ingredients:

3 cloves of garlic, chopped

Chopped parsley

500 grams minced pork

100 grams dry breadcrumb

100 grams of grated cheese

Salt to taste

Ground pepper

3 eggs

Method for preparation:

Pour all the ingredients together in a bowl and mix well, if the mixture seems too hard add half a glass of water.

Let the dough rest for about 30 minutes and then form the meatballs.

Put the meatballs in the almost cooked ragù sauce and cook over low heat for 20 minutes.

HOMEMADE MACCHERONI CALABRESI

Ingredients:
1 kg of flour
1 egg
A few drops of oil
1 pinch of salt
1 glass of water (extra water if needed)
1 knitting needle

Method for preparation:
On a table, pour the flour making a hole in the centre.

Pour the warm water, salt, the egg and oil in the hole and mix well.

When the dough is ready, let it rest for 10 minutes.

Roll out the dough and make dowels of 8 or 10 cm, spiral wrap them around the needle (make sure to roll the needle in some flour first so the pasta doesn't stick), roll them with both hands, then gently pull them out and place them on a floured surface.

Cook them in boiling water with salt and a dash of oil.